Date Due

MAR 6			
OCT 1 7			
NOV. 2 5			
JAN 2			
OCT 1 7			
SEP 2 0			

HE HAD LONG BEEN AWARE OF WHAT HIS TRUE NATURE MUST BE

though he had had the sense not to pass the information on. Now the dream began to grow in him: to find his people!

What was the use of everything he did, when their children must be playing with the same forces as toys, when his greatest discoveries would be as old in their culture as fire in man's? What pride did he have in his achievements, when none of the witless animals who saw them could say "Well done!" as it should be said? What comradeship could he ever know with blind and stupid creatures who soon became as predictable as his machines: *With whom could he think?*

*How weary, flat, stale, and unprofitable
Seem to me all the uses of this world!*

But not of every world! Somewhere, somewhere out among the grand host of the stars . . .

POUL ANDERSON

STRANGERS FROM EARTH

BAEN BOOKS

STRANGERS FROM EARTH

Copyright © 1961 by Poul Anderson

A Baen Book

Baen Publishing Enterprises
260 Fifth Avenue
New York, N.Y. 10001

First Baen printing, March 1987

ISBN: 0-671-65627-9

Cover art by Vincent Di Fate

Printed in the United States of America

Distributed by
SIMON & SCHUSTER
1230 Avenue of the Americas
New York, N.Y. 10020

CONTENTS

Acknowledgments

The following stories reprinted by permission of Scott Meredith Literary Agency, Inc.

Earthman, Beware from *Super Science Stories*, © 1951 by Popular Publications, Inc.

Quixote and the Windmill from *Astounding Science Fiction*, © 1950 by Street and Smith Publications, Inc.

Gypsy from *Astounding Science Fiction*, © 1950 by Street and Smith Publications, Inc.

For the Duration from *Venture Science Fiction*, © 1957 by Fantasy House, Inc.

Duel on Syrtis from *Planet Stories*, © 1951 by Love Romance Publishing Company, Inc.

The Star Beast from *Super Science Stories*, © 1950 by Popular Publications, Inc.

The Disintegrating Sky from *Fantastic Universe*, © 1953 by King-Size Publications, Inc.

Among Thieves from *Astounding Science Fiction*, © 1957 by Street and Smith Publications, Inc.

EARTHMAN, BEWARE!

As he neared the cabin, he grew aware that someone was waiting for him.

He paused for a moment, scowling, and sent his
perceptions ahead to analyze that flash of knowledge. Something in his brain thrilled to the presence of metal, and there were subtler overtones of
the organic—oil and rubber and plastic . . . he
dismissed it as an ordinary small helicopter and
concentrated on the faint, maddeningly elusive
fragments of thought, nervous energy, lifeflows
between cells and molecules. There was only one
person, and the sketchy outline of his data fitted
only a single possibility.

Margaret.

For another instant he stood quietly, and his
primary emotion was sadness. He felt annoyance,
perhaps a subtle dismay that his hiding place had

1

finally been located, but mostly it was pity that
held him. Poor Peggy. Poor kid.

Well—he'd have to have it out. He straightened
his slim shoulders and resumed his walk.

The Alaskan forest was quiet around him. A faint
evening breeze rustled the dark pines and drifted
past his cheeks, a cool lonesome presence in the
stillness. Somewhere birds were twittering as they
settled toward rest, and the mosquitoes raised a
high, thin buzz as they whirled outside the charmed
circle of the odorless repellent he had devised.
Otherwise, there was only the low scrunch of his
footsteps on the ancient floor of needles. After two
years of silence, the vibrations of human presence
were like a great shout along his nerves.

When he came out into the little meadow, the
sun was going down behind the northern hills.
Long aureate rays slanted across the grass, touch-
ing the huddled shack with a wizard glow and
sending enormous shadows before them. The helicopter was a metallic dazzle against the darkling
forest, and he was quite close before his blinded
eyes could discern the woman.

She stood in front of the door, waiting, and the
sunset turned her hair to ruddy gold. She wore
the red sweater and the navy-blue skirt she had
worn when they had last been together, and her
slim hands were crossed before her. So she had
waited for him many times when he came out of
the laboratory, quiet as an obedient child. She had
never turned her pert vivacity on him, not after
noticing how it streamed off his uncomprehending
mind like rain off one of the big pines.

He smiled lopsidedly. "Hullo, Peggy," he said,

feeling the blind inadequacy of words. But what could he say to her?

"Joel . . ." she whispered.

He saw her start and felt the shock along her nerves. His smile grew more crooked, and he nodded. "Yeah," he said. "I've been bald as an egg all my life. Out here, alone, I had no reason to use a wig."

Her wide hazel eyes searched him. He wore backwoodsman's clothes, plaid shirt and stained jeans and heavy shoes, and he carried a fishing rod and tackle box and a string of perch. But he had not changed, at all. The small slender body, the fine-boned ageless features, the luminous dark eyes under the high forehead, they were all the same. Time had laid no finger on him.

Even the very baldness seemed a completion, letting the strong classic arch of his skull stand forth, stripping away another of the layers of ordinariness with which he had covered himself.

He saw that she had grown thin, and it was suddenly too great an effort to smile. "How did you find me, Peggy?" he asked quietly.

From her first word, his mind leaped ahead to the answer, but he let her say it out. "After you'd been gone six months with no word, we—all your friends, insofar as you ever had any—grew worried. We thought maybe something had happened to you in the interior of China. So we started investigating, with the help of the Chinese government, and soon learned you'd never gone there at all. It had just been a red herring, that story about investigating Chinese archeological sites, a blind to gain time while you—disappeared. I just kept on hunting, even after everyone else had given up, and finally Alaska occurred to me. In Nome I picked up rumors of an odd and unfriendly squatter out in the bush. So I came here."

"Couldn't you just have let me stay vanished?" he asked wearily.

"No." Her voice was trembling with her lips. "Not till I knew for sure, Joel. Not till I knew you were safe and—and—"

He kissed her, tasting salt on her mouth, catching the faint fragrance of her hair. The broken waves of her thoughts and emotions washed over him, swirling through his brain in a tide of loneliness and desolation.

Suddenly he knew exactly what was going to happen, what he would have to tell her and the responses she would make—almost to the word, he foresaw it, and the futility of it was like a leaden weight on his mind. But he had to go through with it, every wrenching syllable must come out. Humans were that way, groping through a darkness of solitude, calling to each other across abysses and never, never understanding.

"It was sweet of you," he said awkwardly. "You shouldn't have, Peggy, but it was. . . ." His voice trailed off and his prevision failed. There were no words which were not banal and meaningless.

"I couldn't help it," she whispered. "You know I love you."

"Look, Peggy," he said. "This can't go on. We'll have to have it out now. If I tell you who I am, and why I ran away—" He tried to force cheerfulness. "But never have an emotional scene on an empty stomach. Come on in and I'll fry up these fish."

"I will," she said with something of her old spirit. "I'm a better cook than you."

It would hurt her, but: "I'm afraid you couldn't use my equipment, Peggy."

He signaled to the door, and it opened for him. As she preceded him inside, he saw that her face and hands were red with mosquito bites. She must have been waiting a long time for him to come home.

"Too bad you came today," he said desperately. "I'm usually working in here. I just happened to take today off."

She didn't answer. Her eyes were traveling around the cabin, trying to find the immense order that she knew must underlie its chaos of material.

He had put logs and shingles on the outside to disguise it as an ordinary shack. Within, it might have been his Cambridge laboratory, and she recognized some of the equipment. He had filled a plane with it before leaving. Other things she did not remember, the work of his hands through two lonely years, jungles of wiring and tubing and meters and less understandable apparatus. Only a little of it had the crude, unfinished look of experimental setups. He had been working on some enormous project of his own, and it must be near its end now.

But after that—?

The gray cat which had been his only real companion, even back in Cambridge, rubbed against her legs with a mew that might be recognition. *A friendlier welcome than* he *gave me*, she thought bitterly, and then, seeing his grave eyes on her, flushed. It was unjust. She had hunted him out of his self-chosen solitude and he had been more than decent about it.

Decent—but not human. No unattached human male could have been chased across the world by an attractive woman without feeling more than the quiet regret and pity he showed.

Or did he feel something else? She would never know. No one would ever know all which went on within that beautiful skull. The rest of humanity had too little in common with Joel Weatherfield.

"The *rest* of humanity?" he asked softly.

She started. That old mind-reading trick of his had been enough to alienate most people. You never knew when he would spring it on you, how much of it was guesswork based on a transcendent logic and how much was—was. . . .

He nodded. "I'm partly telepathic," he said, "and I can fill in the gaps for myself—like Poe's Dupin, only better and easier. There are other things involved too—but never mind that for now. Later."

He threw the fish into a cabinet and adjusted several dials on its face. "Supper coming up," he said.

"So now you've invented the robot chef," she said.

"Saves me work."

"You could make another million dollars or so if you marketed it."

"Why? I have more money right now than any reasonable being needs."

"You'd save people a lot of time, you know."

He shrugged.

She looked into a smaller room where he must live. It was sparsely furnished, a cot and a desk and some shelves holding his enormous microprinted library. In one corner stood the multitone instrument with which he composed the music that no one had ever liked or understood. But he had always found the music of man shallow and pointless. And the art of man and the literature of man and all the works and lives of man.

"How's Langtree coming with his new encephalograph?" he asked, though he could guess the answer. "You were going to assist him on it, I recall."

"I don't know." She wondered if her voice reflected her own weariness. "I've been spending all my time looking, Joel."

He grimaced with pain and turned to the automatic cook. A door opened in it and it slid out a tray with two dishes. He put them on a table and gestured to chairs. "Fall to, Peggy."

In spite of herself, the machine fascinated her. "You must have an induction unit to cook that fast," she murmured, "and I suppose your potatoes and greens are stored right inside it. But the mechanical parts—" She shook her head in baffled wonderment, knowing that a blueprint would have revealed some utterly simple arrangement involving only ingenuity.

Dewed cans of beer came out of another cabinet. He grinned and lifted his. "Man's greatest achievement. Skoal."

She hadn't realized she was so hungry. He ate

more slowly, watching her, thinking of the incongruity of Dr. Margaret Logan of M.I.T. wolfing fish and beer in a backwoods Alaskan cabin.

Maybe he should have gone to Mars or some outer-planet satellite. But no, that would have involved leaving a much clearer trail for anyone to follow—you couldn't take off in a spaceship as casually as you could dash over to China. If he had to be found out, he would rather that she did it. For later on she'd keep his secret with the stubborn loyalty he had come to know.

She had always been good to have around, ever since he met her when he was helping M.I.T. on their latest cybernetics work. Twenty-four year old Ph.D.'s with brilliant records were rare enough—when they were also good-looking young women, they became unique. Langtree had been quite hopelessly in love with her, of course. But she had taken on a double program of work, helping Weatherfield at his private laboratories in addition to her usual duties—and she planned to end the latter when her contract expired. She'd been more than useful to him, and he had not been blind to her looks, but it was the same admiration that he had for landscapes and thoroughbred cats and open space. And she had been one of the few humans with whom he could talk at all.

Had been. He exhausted her possibilities in a year, as he drained most people in a month. He had known how she would react to any situation, what she would say to any remark of his, he knew her feelings with a sensitive perception beyond her own knowledge. And the loneliness had returned. But he hadn't anticipated her finding him, he thought wryly. After planning his flight he had not cared—or dared—to follow out all its logical consequences. Well, he was certainly paying for it now, and so was she.

He had cleared the table and put out coffee and cigarets before they began to talk. Darkness veiled the windows, but his fluorotubes came on automatically. She heard the far faint baying of a wolf out in the night, and thought that the forest was less alien to her than this room of machines and the man who sat looking at her with that too brilliant gaze.

He had settled himself in an easy chair and the gray cat had jumped up into his lap and lay purring as his thin fingers stroked its fur. She came over and sat on the stool at his feet, laying one hand on his knee. It was useless to suppress impulses when he knew them before she did.

Joel sighed. "Peggy," he said slowly, "you're making a hell of a mistake."

She thought, briefly, how banal his words were, and then remembered that he had always been awkward in speech. It was as if he didn't feel the ordinary human nuances and had to find his way through society by mechanical rote.

He nodded. "That's right," he said.

"But what's the matter with you?" she protested desperately. "I know they all used to call you 'cold fish' and 'brain-heavy' and 'animated vacuum tube,' but it isn't so. I know you feel more than any of us, only—only—"

"Only not the same way," he finished gently.

"Oh, you always were a strange sort," she said

dully. "The boy wonder, weren't you? Obscure farm kid who entered Harvard at thirteen and graduated with every honor they could give at fifteen. Inventor of the ion-jet space drive, the controlled-disintegration ion process, the cure for the common cold, the crystalline-structure determination of geological age, and only Heaven and the patent office know how much else. Nobel prize winner in physics for your relativistic wave mechanics. Pioneer in a whole new branch of mathematical series theory. Brilliant writer on archeology, economics, ecology, and semantics. Founder of whole new schools in painting and poetry. What's your I.Q., Joel?"

"How should I know? Above 200 or so, I.Q. in the ordinary sense becomes meaningless. I was pretty foolish, Peggy. Most of my published work was done at an early age, out of a childish desire for praise and recognition. Afterward, I couldn't just stop—conditions wouldn't allow it. And of course I had to do something with my time."

"Then at thirty, you pack up and disappear. *Why?*"

"I'd hoped they'd think I was dead," he murmured. "I had a beautiful faked crash in the Gobi, but I guess nobody ever found it. Because poor loyal fools like you just didn't believe I could die. It never occurred to you to look for my remains." His hand passed lightly over her hair, and she sighed and rested her head against his knee. "I should have foreseen that."

"Why in hell I should have fallen in love with a goof like you, I'll never know," she said at last. "Most women ran in fright. Even your money couldn't get them close." She answered her own question with the precision of long thought. "But it was sheer quality, I suppose. After you, everyone else became so trite and insipid." She raised her eyes to him, and there was sudden terrified understanding in them. "And is that why you never married?" she whispered.

He nodded compassionately. Then, slowly, he added, "Also, I'm not too interested in sex yet. I'm still in early adolescence, you know."

"No, I don't know." She didn't move, but he felt her stiffen against him.

"I'm not human," said Joel Weatherfield quietly.

"A mutant? No, you couldn't be." He could feel the tensing of her, the sudden rush of wild thought and wordless nerve current, pulse of blood as the endocrines sought balance on a high taut level of danger. It was the old instinctive dread of the dark and the unknown and the hungry presences beyond a dim circle of firelight—she held herself moveless, but she was an animal bristling in panic.

Calmness came, after a while during which he simply sat stroking her hair. She looked up at him again, forcing herself to meet his eyes.

He smiled as well as he could and said, "No, no, Peggy, all this could never happen in one mutation. I was found in a field of grain one summer morning thirty years ago. A . . . woman . . . who must have been my mother, was lying beside me. They told me later she was of my physical type, and that and the curious iridescent garments she wore made them think she was some circus freak. But she was dead, burned and torn by energies against which she had shielded me with her body.

There were only a few crystalline fragments lying around. The people disposed of that and buried her.

"The Weatherfields were an elderly local couple, childless and kindly. I was only a baby, naturally, and they took me in. I grew quite slowly physically, but of course mentally it was another story. They came to be very proud of me in spite of my odd appearance. I soon devised the perfect toupee to cover my hairlessness, and with that and ordinary clothes I've always been able to pass for human. But you may remember I've never let any human see me without shirt and pants on.

"Naturally, I quickly decided where the truth must lie. Somewhere there must be a race, humanoid but well ahead of man in evolution, which can travel between the stars. Somehow my mother and I had been cast away on this desert planet, and in the vastness of the universe any searchers that there may be have never found us."

He fell back into silence. Presently Margaret whispered, "How—human—are you, Joel?"

"Not very," he said with a flash of the old candid smile she remembered. How often had she seen him look up from some piece of work which was going particularly well and give her just that look! "Here, I'll show you."

He whistled, and the cat jumped from his lap. Another whistle, and the animal was across the room pawing at a switch. Several large plates were released, which the cat carried back in its mouth.

Margaret drew a shaky breath. "I never yet heard of anyone training a cat to run errands."

"This is a rather special cat," he replied absently, and leaned forward to show her the plates. "These are X-rays of myself. You know my technique for photographing different layers of tissue? I developed that just to study myself. I also confess to exhuming my mother's bones, but they proved to be simply a female version of my own. However, a variation of the crystalline-structure method did show that she was at least five hundred years old."

"Five hundred years!"

He nodded. "That's one of several reasons why I'm sure I'm a very young member of my race. Incidentally, her bones showed no sign of age, she corresponded about to a human twenty-five. I don't know whether the natural life span of the race is that great or whether they have artificial means of arresting senility, but I do know that I can expect at least half a millenium of life on Earth. And Earth seems to have a higher gravity than our home world; it's not a very healthy spot for me."

She was too dazed to do more than nod. His finger traced over the X-ray plates. "The skeletal differences aren't too great, but look here and here—the foot, the spine—the skull bones are especially peculiar—Then the internal organs. You can see for yourself that no human being ever had—"

"A double heart?" she asked dully.

"Sort of. It's a single organ, but with more functions than the human heart. Never mind that, it's the neural structure that's most important. Here are several of the brain, taken at different depths and angles."

She fought down a gasp. Her work on encephalography had required a good knowledge of the brain's anatomy. *No human being carries this in his head*.

It wasn't too much bigger than the human. Better organization, she thought; Joel's people would never go insane. There were analogues, a highly convoluted cortex, a medulla, the rest of it. But there were other sections and growths which had no correspondents in any human.

"What are *they?*" she asked.

"I'm not very sure," he replied slowly, a little distastefully. "This one here is what I might call the telepathy center. It's sensitive to neural currents in other organisms. By comparing human reactions and words with the emanations I can detect, I've picked up a very limited degree of telepathy. I can emit, too, but since no human can detect it I've had little use for that power. Then this seems to be for voluntary control of ordinarily involuntary functions—pain blocks, endocrine regulation, and so on—but I've never learned to use it very effectively and I don't dare experiment much on myself. There are other centers—most of them, I don't even know what they're for."

His smile was weary. "You've heard of feral children—the occasional human children who're raised by animals? They never learn to speak, or to exercise any of their specifically human abilities, till they're captured and taught by men. In fact, they're hardly human at all.

"I'm a feral child, Peggy."

She began to cry, deep racking sobs that shook her like a giant's hand. He held her until it passed and she sat again at his knee with the slow tears going down her cheeks. Her voice was a shuddering whisper:

"Oh, my dear, my dear, how lonely you must have been. . . ."

Lonely? No human being would ever know how lonely.

It hadn't been too bad at first. As a child, he had been too preoccupied and delighted with his expanding intellectual horizons to care that the other children bored him—and they, in their turn, heartily disliked Joel for his strangeness and the aloofness they called "snooty." His foster parents had soon learned that normal standards just didn't apply to him, they kept him out of school and bought him the books and equipment he wanted. They'd been able to afford that; at the age of six he had patented, in old Weatherfield's name, improvements on farm machinery that made the family more than well-to-do. He'd always been a "good boy," as far as he was able. They'd had no cause to regret adopting him, but it had been pathetically like the hen who has hatched ducklings and watches them swim away from her.

The years at Harvard had been sheer heaven, an orgy of learning, of conversations and friendship with the great who came to see an equal in the solemn child. He had had no normal social life then either, but he hadn't missed it, the undergraduates were dull and a little frightening. He'd soon learned how to avoid most publicity—after all, infant geniuses weren't altogether unknown. His only real trouble had been with a psychiatrist who wanted him to be more "normal." He grinned as he remembered the rather fiendish ways in which he had frightened the man into leaving him entirely alone.

But toward the end, he had found limitations in the life. It seemed utterly pointless to sit through lectures on the obvious and to turn in assignments of problems which had been done a thousand times before. And he was beginning to find the professors a little tedious, more and more he was able to anticipate their answers to his questions and remarks, and those answers were becoming ever more trite.

He had long been aware of what his true nature must be though he had had the sense not to pass the information on. Now the dream began to grow in him: To find his people!

What was the use of everything he did, when their children must be playing with the same forces as toys, when his greatest discoveries would be as old in their culture as fire in man's? What pride did he have in his achievements, when none of the witless animals who saw them could say "Well done!" as it should be said? What comradeship could he ever know with blind and stupid creatures who soon became as predictable as his machines: *With whom could he think?*

He flung himself savagely into work, with the simple goal of making money. It hadn't been hard. In five years he was a multimillionaire, with agents to relieve him of all the worry and responsibility, with freedom to do as he chose. To work for escape.

How weary, flat, stale, and unprofitable
Seem to me all the uses of this world!

But not of every world! Somewhere, somewhere out among the grand host of the stars. . . .

The long night wore on.

"Why did you come here?" asked Margaret. Her voice was quiet now, muted with hopelessness.

"I wanted secrecy. And human society was getting to be more than I could stand."

She winced, then: "Have you found a way to build a faster-than light spaceship?"

"No. Nothing I've ever discovered indicates any way of getting around Einstein's limitation. There must be a way, but I just can't find it. Not too surprising, really. Our feral child would probably never be able to duplicate ocean-going ships."

"But how do you ever hope to get out of the Solar System, then?"

"I thought of a robot-manned spaceship going from star to star, with myself in suspended animation." He spoke of it as casually as a man might describe some scheme for repairing a leaky faucet. "But it was utterly impractical. My people can't live anywhere near, or we'd have had more indication of them than one shipwreck. They may not live in this galaxy at all. I'll save that idea for a last resort."

"But you and your mother must have been in some kind of ship. Wasn't anything ever found?"

"Just those few glassy fragments I mentioned. It makes me wonder if my people use spaceships at all. Maybe they have some sort of matter transmitter. No, my main hope is some kind of distress signal which will attract help."

"But if they live so many light-years away—"

"I've discovered a strange sort of—well, you might call it radiation, though it has no relation to the electromagnetic spectrum. Energy fields vibrating a certain way produce detectable effects in a similar setup well removed from the first. It's roughly analogous to the old spark-gap radio transmitters. The important thing is that these effects are transmitted with no measurable time lag or diminution with distance."

She would have been aflame with wonder in earlier times. Now she simply nodded. "I see. It's a sort of ultrawave. But if there are no time or distance effects, how can it be traced? It'd be completely nondirectional, unless you could beam it."

"I can't—yet. But I've recorded a pattern of pulses which are to correspond to the arrangement of stars in this part of the galaxy. Each pulse stands for a star, its intensity for the absolute brightness, and its time separation from the other pulses for the distance from the other stars."

"But that's a one-dimensional representation, and space is three dimensional."

"I know. It's not as simple as I said. The problem of such representation was an interesting problem in applied topology—took me a good week to solve. You might be interested in the mathematics, I've got my notes here somewhere—But anyway, my people, when they detect those pulses, should easily be able to deduce what I'm trying to say. I've put Sol at the head of each series of pulses, so they'll even know what particular star it is that I'm at. Anyway, there can only be one or a few configurations exactly like this in the universe, so I've given them a fix. I've set up an apparatus to broadcast my call automatically. Now I can only wait."

"How long have you waited?"

He scowled. "A good year now—and no sign. I'm getting worried. Maybe I should try something else."

"Maybe they don't use your ultrawave at all. It might be obsolete in their culture."

He nodded. "It could well be. But what else is there?"

She was silent.

Presently Joel stirred and sighed. "That's the story, Peggy."

She nodded, mutely.

"Don't feel sorry for me," he said. "I'm doing all right. My research here is interesting. I like the country, I'm happier than I've been for a long time."

"That's not saying much, I'm afraid," she answered.

"No, but—Look, Peggy, you know what I am now. A monster. More alien to you than an ape. It shouldn't be hard to forget me."

"Harder than you think, Joel. I love you. I'll always love you."

"But—Peggy, it's ridiculous. Just suppose that I did come live with you. There could never be children . . . but I suppose that doesn't matter too much. We'd have nothing in common, though. Not a thing. We couldn't talk, we couldn't share any of the million little things that make a marriage, we could hardly ever work together. I can't live in human society any more, you'd soon lose all your friends, you'd become as lonely as I. And in the end you'd grow old, your powers would fade and die, and I'd still be approaching my maturity. Peggy, neither of us could stand it."

"I know."

"Langtree is a fine man. It'd be easy to love him. You've no right to withhold a heredity as magnificent as yours from your race."

"You may be right."

He put a hand under her chin and tilted her face up to his. "I have some powers over the mind," he said slowly. "With your cooperation, I could adjust your feelings about this."

She tensed back from him, her eyes wide and frightened. "No—"

"Don't be a fool. It would only be doing now what time will do anyway." His smile was tired, crooked. "I'm really a remarkably easy person to forget, Peggy."

His will was too strong. It radiated from him, in the lambent eyes and the delicately carved features that were almost human, it pulsed in great drowsy waves from his telepathic brain and seemed almost to flow through the thin hands. Useless to resist, futile to deny—give up, give up and sleep. She was so tired.

She nodded, finally. Joel smiled the old smile she knew so well. He began to talk.

She never remembered the rest of the night, save as a blur of half awareness, a soft voice that whispered in her head, a face dimly seen through wavering mists. Once, she recalled, there was a machine that clicked and hummed, and little lights flashing and spinning in darkness. Her memory was stirred, roiled like a quiet pool, things she had forgotten through most of her life floated to the surface. It seemed as if her mother was beside her.

In the vague foggy dawn, he let her go. There was a deep unhuman calm in her, she looked at him with something of a sleepwalker's empty stare and her voice was flat. It would pass, she would soon become normal again, but Joel Weatherfield would be a memory with little emotional color, a ghost somewhere in the back of her mind.

A ghost. He felt utterly tired, drained of strength and will. He didn't belong here, he was a shadow that should have been flitting between the stars, the sunlight of Earth erased him.

"Good-by, Peggy," he said. "Keep my secret. Don't let anyone know where I am. And good luck go with you all your days."

"Joel—" She paused on the doorstep, a puzzled frown crossing her features. "Joel, if you can think at me that way, can't your people do the same?"

"Of course. What of it?" For the first time, he didn't know what was coming, he had changed her too much for prediction.

"Just that—why should they bother with gadgets like your ultrawave for talking to each other? They should be able to think between the stars."

He blinked. It had occurred to him, but he had not thought much beyond it, he had been too preoccupied with his work.

"Good-by, Joel." She turned and walked away through the dripping gray fog. An early sunbeam struck through a chance rift and glanced off her hair. He stood in the doorway until she was gone.

He slept through most of the day. Awakening, he began to think over what had been said.

By all that was holy, Peggy was right! He had immersed himself too deeply in the purely technical problems of the ultrawave, and since then in mathematical research which passed the time of waiting, to stand off and consider the basic logic of the situation. But this—it made sense.

He had only the vaguest notion of the inherent powers of his own mind. Physical science had offered too easy an outlet for him. Nor could he, unaided, hope to get far in such studies. A human feral child might have the heredity of a mathematical genius, but unless he was found and taught by his own kind he would never comprehend the elements of arithmetic—or of speech or sociability or any of the activities which set man off from the other animals. There was just too long a heritage of prehuman and early human development for one man, alone, to recapitulate in a lifetime, when his environment held no indication of the particular road his ancestors had taken.

But those idle nerves and brain centers must be for something. He suspected that they were means of direct control over the most basic forces in the universe. Telepathy, telekinesis, precognition—what godlike heritage had been denied him?

At any rate, it did seem that his race had gone beyond the need of physical mechanisms. With complete understanding of the structure of the space-time-energy continuum, with control by direct will of its underlying processes, they would project themselves or their thoughts from star to star, create what they needed by sheer thought—and pay no attention to the gibberings of lesser races.

Fantastic, dizzying prospect! He stood breathless before the great shining vision that opened to his eyes.

He shook himself back to reality. The immediate problem was getting in touch with his race. That meant a study of the telepathic energies he had hitherto almost ignored.

He plunged into a fever of work. Time became meaningless, a succession of days and nights, waning light and drifting snow and the slow return of spring. He had never had much except his work to live for, now it devoured the last of his thoughts. Even during the periods of rest and exercise he forced himself to take, his mind was still at the problem, gnawing at it like a dog with a bone. And slowly, slowly, knowledge grew.

Telepathy was not directly related to the brain pulses measured by encephalography. Those were feeble, short-range by-products of neuronic activity. Telepathy, properly controlled, leaped over an intervening space with an arrogant ignoring of time. It was, he decided, another part of what he had labeled the ultrawave spectrum, which was related to gravitation as an effect of the geometry of space-time. But, while gravitational effects were produced by the presence of matter, ultra-wave effects came into being when certain energy fields vibrated. However, they did not appear unless there was a properly tuned receiver somewhere. They seemed somehow "aware" of a listener even before they came into existence. That suggested fascinating speculations about the nature of time, but he turned away from it. His people would know more about it than he could ever find out alone.

But the concept of waves was hardly applicable to something that traveled with an "infinite velocity" —poor term semantically, but convenient. He could assign an ultrawave a frequency, that of the generating energy fields, but then the wavelength would be infinite. Better to think of it in terms of tensors, and drop all pictorial analogies.

His nervous system did not itself contain the ultraenergies. Those were omnipresent, inherent in the very structure of the cosmos. But his telepathy centers, properly trained, were somehow coupled to that great underlying flow; they could impose the desired vibrations on it. Similarly, he supposed, his other centers could control those forces to create or destroy or move matter, to cross space, to scan the past and future probability-worlds, to. . . .

He couldn't do it himself. He just couldn't find out enough in even his lifetime. Were he literally immortal, he might still never learn what he had to know; his mind had been trained into human thought patterns, and this was something that lay beyond man's power of comprehension.

But all I need is to send one clear call. . . .

He struggled with it. Through the endless winter nights he sat in the cabin and fought to master his brain. How did you send a shout to the stars?

Tell me, feral child, how do you solve a partial differential equation?

Perhaps some of the answer lay in his own mind. The brain has two types of memory, the "permanent" and the "circulating," and apparently the former kind is never lost. It recedes into the subconscious, but it is still there, and it can be brought out again. As a child, a baby, he would have observed things, remembered sights of apparatus and feelings of vibrations, which his more mature mind could now analyze.

He practiced autohypnosis, using a machine he devised to help him, and the memories came back, memories of warmth and light and great pulsing forces. Yes—yes, there was an engine of some sort, he could see it thrumming and flickering before him. It took a while before he could translate the infant's alien impressions into his present sensory evaluations, but when that job was done he had a clear picture of—something.

That helped, just a little. It suggested certain types of hookup, empirical patterns which had not occurred to him before. And now slowly, slowly, he began to make progress.

An ultrawave demands a receiver for its very existence. So he could not flash a thought to any of his people unless one of them happened to be listening on that particular "wave"—its pattern of frequency, modulation, and other physical characteristics. And his untrained mind simply did not send on that "band." He couldn't do it, he couldn't imagine the wave-form of his race's normal thought. He was faced with a problem similar to that of a

man in a foreign country who must invent its
language for himself before he can communicate—
without even being allowed to listen to it, and
knowing only that its phonetic, grammatical, and
semantic values are entirely different from those of
his native speech.

Insoluble? No, maybe not. His mind lacked the
power to send a call out through the stars, lacked
the ability to make itself intelligible. But a machine has no such limitations.

He could modify his ultrawave; it already had
the power, and he could give it the coherence.
For he could insert a random factor in it, a device
which would vary the basic wave-form in every
conceivable permutation of characteristics, running through millions or billions of tries in a
second—and the random wave could be modu-
lated, too, his own thoughts could be superimposed. Whenever the machine found resonance
with anything that could receive—anything, literally, for millions of light-years—an ultrawave would
be generated and the random element cut off. Joel
could stay on that band then, examining it at his
leisure.

Sooner or later, one of the bands he hit would
be that of his race. And he would know it.

The device, when he finished, was crude and
ugly, a great ungainly thing of tangled wires and
gleaming tubes and swirling cosmic energies. One
lead from it connected to a metal band around his
own head, imposing his basic ultrawave pattern on
the random factor and feeding back whatever was
received into his brain. He lay on his bunk, with a

control panel beside him, and started the machine working.

Vague mutterings, sliding shadows, strangeness rising out of the roiled depths of his mind. . . . He grinned thinly, battling down the cold apprehension which rose in his abused nerves, and began experimenting with the machine. He wasn't too sure of all its characteristics himself, and it would take a while too before he had full control of his thought-pattern.

Silence, darkness, and now and then a glimpse, a brief blinding instant when the random gropings struck some basic resonance and a wave sprang into being and talked to his brain. Once he looked through Margaret's eyes, across a table to Langtree's face. There was candlelight, he remembered afterward, and a small string orchestra was playing in the background. Once he saw the ragged outlines of a city men had never built, rising up toward a cloudy sky while a strangely slow and heavy sea lapped against its walls.

Once, too, he did catch a thought flashing between the stars. But it was no thought of his kind, it was a great white blaze like a sun exploding in his head, and cold, cold. He screamed aloud, and for a week afterward dared not resume his experiments.

In the springtime dusk, he found his answer.

The first time, the shock was so great that he lost contact again. He lay shaking, forcing calm on himself, trying to reproduce the exact pattern his own brain, as well as the machine, had been sending. Easy, easy—The baby's mind had been drifting in a mist of dreams, *thus*. . . .

The baby. For his groping, uncontrollable brain could not resonate with any of the superbly trained adult minds of his people.

But a baby has no spoken language. Its mind slides amorphously from one pattern to another, there are no habits as yet to fix it, and one tongue is as good as any other. By the laws of randomness, Joel had struck the pattern which an infant of his race happened to be giving out at the moment.

He found it again, and the tingling warmth of contact flowed into him, deliciously, marvelously, a river in a dusty desert, a sun warming the chill of the solipsistic loneliness in which humans wandered from their births to the end of their brief meaningless lives. He fitted his mind to the baby's, let the two streams of consciousness flow into one, a river running toward the mighty sea of the race.

The feral child crept out of the forest. Wolves howled at his back, the hairy four-footed brothers of cave and chase and darkness, but he heard them not. He bent over the baby's cradle, the tangled hair falling past his gaunt witless face, and looked with a dim stirring of awe and wonder. The baby spread its hand, a little soft starfish, and his own gnarled fingers, stole toward it, trembling at the knowledge that this was a paw like his own.

Now he had only to wait until some adult looked into the child's mind. It shouldn't be long, and meanwhile he rested in the timeless drowsy peace of the very young.

Somewhere in the outer cosmos, perhaps on a planet swinging about a sun no one of Earth would ever see, the baby rested in a cradle of warm, pulsing forces. He did not have a room around him, there was a shadowiness which no human could ever quite comprehend, lit by flashes of the energy that created the stars.

The baby sensed the nearing of something that meant warmth and softness, sweetness in his mouth and murmuring in his mind. He cooed with delight, reaching his hands out into the shaking twilight of the room. His mother's mind ran ahead of her, folding about the little one.

A scream!

Frantically, Joel reached for her mind, flashing and flashing the pattern of location-pulses through the baby's brain into hers. He lost her, his mind fell sickeningly in on itself—no, no, someone else was reaching for him now, analyzing the pattern of the machine and his own wild oscillations and fitting smoothly into them.

A deep, strong voice in his brain, somehow unmistakably male—Joel relaxed, letting the other mind control his, simply emitting his signals.

It would take—them—a little while to analyze the meaning of his call. Joel lay in a half conscious state, aware of one small part of the being's mind maintaining a thread of contact with him while the rest reached out, summoning others across the universe, calling for help and information.

So he had won. Joel thought of Earth, dreamily and somehow wistfully. Odd that in this moment of triumph his mind should dwell on the little things he was leaving behind—an Arizona sunset, a nightingale under the moon, Peggy's flushed face bent over an instrument beside his. Beer and music and windy pines.

But O my people! Never more to be lonely. . . .

Decision. A sensation of falling, rushing down a vortex of stars toward Sol—approach!

The being would have to locate him on Earth. Joel tried to picture a map, though the thought-patterns that corresponded in his brain to a particular visualization would not make sense to the other. But in some obscure way, it might help.

Maybe it did. Suddenly the telepathic band snapped, but there was a rush of other impulses, life forces like flame, the nearness of a god. Joel stumbled gasping to his feet and flung open the door.

The moon was rising above the dark hills, a hazy light over trees and patches of snow and the wet ground. The air was chill and damp, sharp in his lungs.

The being who stood there, outlined in the radiance of his garments, was taller than Joel, an adult. His grave eyes were too brilliant to meet, it was as if the life within him were incandescent. And when the full force of his mind reached out, flowing over and into Joel, running along every nerve and cell of him. . . .

He cried out with the pain of it and fell to his hands and knees. The intolerable force lightened, faded to a thrumming in his brain that shook every fiber of it. He was being studied, analyzed, no tiniest part of him was hidden from those terrible eyes and from the logic that recreated more of him than he knew himself. His own distorted telepathic language was at once intelligible to the watcher, and he croaked his appeal.

The answer held pity, but it was as remote and inexorable as the thunders on Olympus.

Child, it is too late. Your mother must have been caught in a—?—energy vortex and caused to—?—on Earth, and now you have been raised by the animals.

Think, child. Think of the feral children of this native race. When they were restored to their own kind, did they become human? No, it was too late. The basic personality traits are determined in the first years of childhood, and their specifically human attributes, unused, had atrophied.

It is too late, too late. Your mind has become too fixed in rigid and limited patterns. Your body has made a different adjustment from that which is necessary to sense and control the forces we use. You even need a machine to speak.

You no longer belong to our race.

Joel lay huddled on the ground, shaking, not thinking or daring to think.

The thunders rolled through his head: *We cannot have you interfering with the proper mental training of our children. And since you can never rejoin your kind, but must make the best adaptation you can to the race you live with, the kindest as well as the wisest thing for us to do is to make certain changes. Your memory and that of others, your body, the work you are doing and have done—*

There were others filling the night, the gods come to Earth, shining and terrible beings who lifted each fragment of experience he had ever had out of him and made their judgments on it. Darkness closed over him, and he fell endlessly into oblivion.

*   *   *

He awoke in his bed, wondering why he should be so tired.

Well, the cosmic-ray research had been a hard and lonely grind. Thank heaven and his lucky stars it was over! He'd take a well-earned vacation at home now. It'd be good to see his friends again— and Peggy.

Dr. Joel Weatherfield, eminent young physicist, rose cheerfully and began making ready to go home.

QUIXOTE AND THE WINDMILL

The first robot in the world came walking over green hills with sunlight aflash off his polished metal hide. He walked with a rippling grace that was almost feline, and his tread fell noiselessly— but you could feel the ground vibrate ever so faintly under the impact of that terrific mass, and the air held a subliminal quiver from the great engine that pulsed within him.

Him. You could not think of the robot as neuter. He had the brutal maleness of a naval rifle or a blast furnace. All the smooth silent elegance of perfect design and construction did not hide the weight and strength of a two and a half-meter height. His eyes glowed, as if with inner fires of smoldering atoms, they could see in any frequency range he selected, he could turn an X-ray beam on you and look you through and through with those

33

terrible eyes. They had built him humanoid, but
had had the good taste not to give him a face;
there were the eyes, with their sockets for extra
lenses when he needed microscopic or telescopic
vision, and there were a few other small sensory
and vocal orifices, but otherwise his head was a
mask of shining metal. Humanoid, but not human—
man's creation, but more than man—the first independent, volitional, nonspecialized machine—
but they had dreamed of him, long ago, he had
once been the jinni in the bottle or the Golem,
Bacon's brazen head or Frankenstein's monster,
the man-transcending creature who could serve or
destroy with equal contemptuous ease.

He walked under a bright summer sky, over
sunlit fields and through little groves that danced
and whispered in the wind. The houses of men
were scattered here and there, the houses which
practically took care of themselves; over beyond
the horizon was one of the giant, almost automatic
food factories; a few self-piloting carplanes went
quietly overhead. Humans were in sight, sun-
browned men and their women and children going
about their various errands with loose bright garments floating in the breeze. A few seemed to be
at work, there was a colorist experimenting with a
new chromatic harmony, a composer sitting on his
verandah striking notes out of an omniplayer, a
group of engineers in a transparent-walled laboratory testing some mechanisms. But with the standard work period what it was these days, most
were engaged in recreation. A picnic, a dance under
trees, a concert, a pair of lovers, a group of children in one of the immemorially ancient games of

their age-group, an old man happily enhammocked with a book and a bottle of beer—the human race was taking it easy.

They saw the robot go by, and often a silence fell as his tremendous shadow slipped past. His electronic detectors sensed the eddying pulses that meant nervousness, a faint unease—oh, they trusted the cybernetics men, they didn't look for a devouring monster, but they wondered. They felt man's old unsureness of the alien and unknown, deep in their minds they wondered what the robot was about and what his new and invincible race might mean to Earth's dwellers—then, perhaps, as his gleaming height receded over the hills, they laughed and forgot him.

The robot went on.

There were not many customers in the Casanova at this hour. After sunset the tavern would fill up and the autodispensers would be kept busy, for it had a good live-talent show and television was becoming unfashionable. But at the moment only those who enjoyed a mid-afternoon glass, together with some serious drinkers, were present.

The building stood alone on a high wooded ridge, surrounded by its gardens and a good-sized parking lot. Its colonnaded exterior was long and low and gracious; inside it was cool and dim and fairly quiet; and the general air of decorum, due entirely to lack of patronage, would probably last till evening. The manager had gone off on his own business and the girls didn't find it worthwhile to be around till later, so the Casanova was wholly in the charge of its machines.

Two men were giving their autodispenser a good workout. It could hardly deliver one drink before a coin was given it for another. The smaller man was drinking whiskey and soda, the larger one stuck to the most potent available ale, and both were already thoroughly soused.

They sat in a corner booth from which they could look out the open door, but their attention was directed to the drinks. It was one of those curious barroom acquaintances which spring up between utterly diverse types. They would hardly remember each other the next day. But currently they were exchanging their troubles.

The little dark-haired fellow, Roger Brady, finished his drink and dialed for another. "Beatcha!" he said triumphantly.

"Gimme time," said the big red-head, Pete Borklin. "This stuff goes down slower."

Brady got out a cigarette. His fingers shook as he brought it to his mouth and puffed it into lighting. "Why can't that drink come right away?" he mumbled. "I resent a ten-second delay. Ten dry eternities! I demand instantaneously mixed drinks, delivered faster than light."

The glass arrived, and he raised it to his lips. "I am afraid," he said, with the careful precision of a very drunk man, "that I am going on a weeping jag. I would much prefer a fighting jag. But unfortunately there is nobody to fight."

"I'll fight you," offered Borklin. His huge fists closed.

"Nah—why? Wouldn't be a fight, anyway. You'd just mop me up. And why should we fight? We're both in the same boat."

"Yeah." Borklin looked at his fists. "Not much use, anyway," he said. "Somebody'd do a lot better job o' killing with an autogun than I could with—these." He unclenched them, slowly, as if with an effort, and took another drag at his glass.

"What we want to do," said Brady, "is to fight a world. We want to blow up all Earth and scatter the pieces from here to Pluto. Only it wouldn't do any good, Pete. Some machine'd come along and put it back together again."

"I just wanna get drunk," said Borklin. "My wife left me. D'I tell you that? My wife left me."

"Yeah, you told me."

Borklin shook his heavy head, puzzled. "She said I was a drunk. I went to a doctor like she said, but it didn't help none. He said . . . I forget what he said. But I had to keep on drinking anyway. Wasn't anything else to do."

"I know. Psychiatry helps people solve problems. It's not being able to solve a problem that drives a man insane. But when the problem is inherently insoluble—what then? One can only drink, and try to forget."

"My wife wanted me to amount to something," said Borklin. "She wanted me to get a job. But what could I do? I tried. Honest, I tried. I tried for . . . well, I've been trying all my life, really. There just wasn't any work around. Not any I could do."

"Fortunately, the basic citizen's allowance is enough to get drunk on," said Brady. "Only the drinks don't arrive fast enough. I demand an instantaneous autodispenser."

Borklin dialed for another ale. He looked at his

hands in a bewildered way. "I've always been strong," he said. "I know I'm not bright, but I'm strong, and I'm good at working with machines and all. But nobody would hire me." He spread his thick workman's fingers. "I was handy at home. We had a little place in Alaska, my dad didn't hold with too many gadgets, so I was handy around there. But he's dead now, the place is sold, what good are my hands?"

"The worker's paradise." Brady's thin lips twisted. "Since the end of the Transition, Earth has been Utopia. Machines do all the routine work, *all* of it, they produce so much that the basic necessities of life are free."

"The hell. They want money for everything."

"Not much. And you get your citizen's allowance, which is just a convenient way of making your needs free. When you want more money, for the luxuries, you work, as an engineer or scientist or musician or painter or tavern keeper or spaceman or . . . anything there's a demand for. You don't work too hard. Paradise!" Brady's shaking fingers spilled cigarette ash on the table. A little tube dipped down from the wall and sucked it up.

"I can't find work. They don't want me. Nowhere."

"Of course not. What earthly good is manual labor these days? Machines do it all. Oh, there are technicians to be sure, quite a lot of them—but they're all highly skilled men, years of training. The man who has nothing to offer but his strength and a little rule-of-thumb ingenuity doesn't get work. There *is* no place for him!" Brady took another swallow from his glass. "Human genius has eliminated the need for the workman. Now it only remains to eliminate the workman himself."

Borklin's fists closed again, dangerously. "Whattayuh mean?" he asked harshly. "Whattayuh mean, anyway?"

"Nothing personal. But you know it yourself. Your type no longer fits into human society. So the geneticists are gradually working it out of the race. The population is kept static, relatively small, and is slowly evolving toward a type which can adapt to the present en . . . environment. And that's not your type, Pete."

The big man's anger collapsed into futility. He stared emptily at his glass. "What to do?" he whispered. "What can I do?"

"Not a thing, Pete. Just drink, and try to forget your wife. Just drink."

"Mebbe they'll get out to the stars."

"Not in our lifetimes. And even then, they'll want to take their machines along. We still won't be any more useful. Drink up, old fellow. Be glad! You're living in Utopia!"

There was silence then, for a while. The day was bright outside. Brady was grateful for the obscurity of the tavern.

Borklin said at last: "What I can't figure is you. You look smart. You can fit in . . . can't you?"

Brady grinned humorously. "No, Pete. I had a job, yes. I was a mediocre servotechnician. The other day I couldn't take any more. I told the boss what to do with his servos, and I've been drinking ever since. I don't think I ever want to stop."

"But how come?"

"Dreary, routine—I hated it. I'd rather stay tight.

I had psychiatric help, too, of course, and it didn't do me any good. The same insoluble problem as yours, really."

"I don't get it."

"I'm a bright boy, Pete. Why hide it? My I.Q. puts me in the genius class. But—not quite bright enough." Brady fumbled for another coin. He could only find a bill, but the machine gave him change. "I want inshantaneous auto . . . or did I say that before? Never mind. It doesn't matter." He buried his face in his hands.

"How do you mean, not quite bright enough?" Borklin was insistent. He had a vague notion that a new slant on his own problem might conceivably help him see a solution. "That's what they told me, only politer. But you—"

"I'm too bright to be an ordinary technician. Not for long. And I have none of the artistic or literary talent which counts so highly nowadays. What I wanted was to be a mathematician. All my life I wanted to be a mathematician. And I worked at it. I studied. I learned all any human head could hold, and I know where to look up the rest." Brady grinned wearily. "So what's the upshot? The mathematical machines have taken over. Not only all routine computation—that's old—but even independent research. At a higher level than the human brain can operate.

"They still have humans working at it. Sure. They have men who outline the problems, control and check the machines, follow through all the steps—men who are the . . . the soul of the science, even today.

"*But*—only the top-flight geniuses. The really

brilliant, original minds, with flashes of sheer inspiration. *They* are still needed. But the machines do all the rest."

Brady shrugged. "I'm not a first-rank genius, Pete. I can't do anything that an electronic brain can't do quicker and better. So I didn't get my job, either."

They sat quiet again. Then Borklin said, slowly: "At least you can get some fun. I don't like all these concerts and pictures and all that fancy stuff. I don't have more than drinking and women and maybe some stereofilm."

"I suppose you're right," said Brady indifferently. "But I'm not cut out to be a hedonist. Neither are you. We both *want* to work. We want to feel we have some importance and value—we want to amount to something. Our friends . . . your wife . . . I had a girl once, Pete . . . we're expected to amount to something.

"Only there's nothing for us to do—"

A hard and dazzling sun-flash caught his eye. He looked out through the door, and jerked with a violence that upset his drink.

"Great universe!" he breathed. "Pete . . . Pete . . . look, it's the robot! *It's the robot!*"

"Huh?" Borklin twisted around, trying to focus his eyes out the door. "Whazzat?"

"The robot—you've heard of it, man." Brady's soddenness was gone in a sudden shivering intensity. His voice was like metal. "They built him three years ago at Cybernetics Lab. Manlike, with a volitional, nonspecialized brain—manlike, but more than man!"

"Yeah . . . yeah, I heard." Borklin looked out

and saw the great shining form striding across the gardens, bound on some unknown journey that took him past the tavern. "They were testing him. But he's been running around loose for a year or so now— Wonder where he's going?"

"I don't know." As if hypnotized, Brady looked after the mighty thing. "I don't know—" His voice trailed off, then suddenly he stood up and then lashed out: "But we'll find out! Come on, Pete!"

"Where . . . huh . . . why—" Borklin rose slowly, fumbling through his own bewilderment. "What do you mean?"

"Don't you see, don't you see? It's *the robot*— the man after man—all that man is and how much more we don't even imagine. Pete, the machines have been replacing men, here, there, everywhere. This is the machine that will replace *man!*"

Borklin said nothing, but trailed out after Brady. The smaller man kept on talking, rapidly, bitterly: "Sure—why not? Man is simply flesh and blood. Humans are only human. They're not efficient enough for our shiny new world. Why not scrap the whole human race? How long till we have nothing but men of metal in a meaningless metal ant-heap."

"Come on, Pete. Man is going down into darkness. But we can go down fighting!"

Something of it penetrated Borklin's mind. He saw the towering machine ahead of him, and suddenly it was as if it embodied all which had broken him. The ultimate machine, the final arrogance of efficiency, remote and godlike and indifferent as it smashed him—suddenly he hated it with a violence that seemed to split his skull apart. He lumbered clumsily beside Brady and they caught up with the robot together.

"Turn around!" called Brady. "Turn around and fight!"

The robot paused. Brady picked up a stone and threw it. The rock bounced off the armor with a dull clang.

The robot faced about. Borklin ran at him, cursing. His heavy shoes kicked at the robot's ankle joints, his fists battered at the front. They left no trace.

"Stop that," said the robot. His voice had little tonal variation, but there was the resonance of a great bell in it. "Stop that. You will injure yourself."

Borklin retreated, gasping with the pain of bruised flesh and smothering impotence. Brady reeled about to stand before the robot. The alcohol was singing and buzzing in his head, but his voice came oddly clear.

"We can't hurt you," he said. "We're Don Quixote, tilting at windmills. But you wouldn't know about that. You wouldn't know about any of man's old dreams."

"I am unable to account for your present actions," said the robot. His eyes blazed with their deep fires, searching the men. Unconsciously, they shrank away a little.

"You are unhappy," decided the robot. "You have been drinking to escape your own unhappiness, and in your present intoxication you identify me with the causes of your misery."

"Why not?" flared Brady. "Aren't you? The machines are taking over all Earth with their smug efficiency, making man a parasite—and now you come, the ultimate machine, you're the one who's going to replace man himself."

"I have no belligerent intentions," said the robot. "You should know I was conditioned against any such tendencies, even while my brain was in process of construction." Something like a chuckle vibrated in the deep metal voice. "What reason do I have to fight anyone?"

"None," said Brady thinly. "None at all. You'll just take over, as more and more of you are made, as your emotionless power begins to—"

"Begins to what?" asked the robot. "And how do you know I am emotionless? Any psychologist will tell you that emotion, though not necessarily of the human type, is a basic of thought. What logical reason does a being have to think, to work, even to exist? It cannot rationalize its so doing, it simply does, because of its endocrine system, its power plant, whatever runs it . . . its emotions! And any mentality capable of self-consciousness will feel as wide a range of emotion as you—it will be as happy or as interested—or as miserable—as you!"

It was weird, even in a world used to machines that were all but alive, thus to stand and argue with a living mass of metal and plastic, vacuum and energy. The strangeness of it struck Brady, he realized just how drunk he was. But still he had to snarl his hatred and despair out, mouth any phrases at all just so they relieved some of the bursting tension within him.

"I don't care how you feel or don't feel," he said, stuttering a little now. "It's that you're the future, the meaningless future when all men are as useless as I am now, and I hate you for it and the worst of it is I can't kill you."

The robot stood like a burnished statue of some old and non-anthropomorphic god, motionless, but his voice shivered the quiet air: "Your case is fairly common. You have been relegated to obscurity by advanced technology. But do not identify yourself with all mankind. There will always be men who think and dream and sing and carry on all the race has ever loved. The future belongs to them, not to you—or to me.

"I am surprised that a man of your apparent intelligence does not realize my position. But—what earthly good is a robot? By the time science had advanced to the point where I could be built, there was no longer any reason for it. Think—you have a specialized machine to perform or help man perform every conceivable task. What possible use is there for a nonspecialized machine to do them all? Man himself fulfills that function, and the machines are no more than his tools. Does a housewife want a robot servant when she need only control the dozen machines which already do all the work? Why should a scientist want a robot that could, say, go into dangerous radioactive rooms when he has already installed automatic and remote-controlled apparatus which does everything there? And surely the artists and thinkers and policy-makers don't need robots, they are performing specifically human tasks, it will always be *man* who sets man's goals and dreams his dreams. The all-purpose machine is and forever will be—man himself.

"Man, I was made for purely scientific study.

After a couple of years they had learned all there was to learn about me—and I had no other purpose! They let me become a harmless, aimless, meaningless wanderer, just so I could be doing something—and my life is estimated at five hundred years!

"I have no purpose. I have no real reason for existence. I have no companion, no place in human society, no use for my strength and my brain. Man, man, do you think *I* am happy?"

The robot turned to go. Brady was sitting on the grass, holding his head to keep it from whirling off into space, so he didn't see the giant metal god depart. But he caught the last words flung back, and somehow there was such a choking bitterness in the toneless brazen voice that he could never afterward forget them.

"Man, you are the lucky one. *You* can get drunk!"

GYPSY

From afar, I caught a glimpse of the *Traveler* as my boat swung toward the planet. The great spaceship looked like a toy at that distance, a frail bubble of metal and air and energy against the enormous background of space. I thought of the machines within her, humming and whirring and clicking very faintly as they pursued their unending round of services, making that long hull into a living world—the hull that was now empty of life—and I had a sudden odd feeling of sympathy. As if she were alive, I felt that the *Traveler* was lonely.

The planet swelled before me, a shining blue shield blazoned with clouds and continents, rolling against a limitless dark and the bitterly burning stars. Harbor, we had named that world, the harbor at the end of our long journey, and there were few lovelier names. Harbor, haven, rest and peace

47

and a sky overhead as roof against the naked blaze of space. It was good to get home.

I searched the heavens for another glimpse of the *Traveler*, but I couldn't find her tiny form in that thronging wilderness of stars. No matter, she was still on her orbit about Harbor, moored to the planet, perhaps forever. I concentrated on bringing the spaceboat down.

Atmosphere whistled about the hull. After a month in the gloom and poisonous cold of the fifth planet, alone among utterly unhuman natives, I was usually on fire to get home and brought my craft down with a recklessness that overloaded the gravity beams. But this time I went a little more carefully, telling myself that I'd rather be late for supper than not arrive at all. Or perhaps it was that brief chance vision of the *Traveler* which made me suddenly thoughtful. After all, we had had some good times aboard her.

I sent the boat slanting toward the peninsula in the north temperate zone on which most of us were settled. The outraged air screamed behind me as I slammed down on the hard-packed earth that served us for a landing field. There were a few warehouses and service shops around it, long low buildings of the heavy timbers used by most of the colonists, and a couple of private homes a kilometer or so away. But otherwise only long grass rustled in the wind, gardens and wild groves, sunlight streaming out of a high blue sky. When I stepped from the boat, the fresh vivid scent of the land fairly leaped to meet me. I could hear the sea growling beyond the horizon.

Tokogama was on duty at the field. He was

sitting on the porch of the office, smoking his pipe and watching the clouds sail by overhead, but he greeted me with the undemonstrative cordiality of old friends who know each other too well to need many words.

"So that's the portmaster," I said. "Soft touch. All you have to do is puff that vile-smelling thing and say hello to me."

"That's all," he admitted cheerfully. "I am retained only for my uncommonly high ornamental value."

It was, approximately, true. Our aircraft used the field with no formality, and we only kept this one space vessel in operation. The portmaster was on hand simply to oversee servicing and in the unlikely case of some emergency or dispute. But none of the colony's few public posts—captain, communications officer, and the rest—required much effort in as simple a society as ours, and they were filled as spare-time occupations by anyone who wanted them. There was no compensation except getting first turn at using the machinery for farming or heavy construction which we owned in common.

"How was the trip?" asked Tokogama.

"Pretty good," I said. "I gave them our machines and they filled my holds with their ores and alloys. And I managed to take a few more notes on their habits, and establish a few more code symbols for communication."

"Which is a very notable brick added to the walls of science, but in view of the fact that you're the only one who ever goes there it really makes no odds." Tokogama's dark eyes regarded me curiously. "Why do you keep on making those trips out there, Erling? Quite a few of the other boys wouldn't mind visiting Five once in a while. Will and Ivan both mentioned it to me last week."

"I'm no hog," I said. "If either of them, or anyone else, wants a turn at the trading job, let 'em learn space piloting and they can go. But meanwhile—I like the work. You know that I was one of those who voted to continue the search for Earth."

Tokogama nodded. "So you were. But that was three years ago. Even you must have grown some roots here."

"Oh, I have," I laughed. "Which reminds me I'm hungry, and judging by the sun it's the local dinner time. So I'll get on home, if Alanna knows I'm back."

"She can't help it," he smiled. "The whole continent knows when you're back, the way you rip the atmosphere coming in. That home cooking must have a powerful magnetic attraction."

"A steak aroma of about fifty thousand gauss—" I turned to go, calling over my shoulder: "Why don't you come to dinner tomorrow evening? I'll invite the other boys and we'll have an old-fashioned hot air session."

"I was sort of hinting in that direction," said Tokogama.

I got my carplane out of the hangar and took off with a whisper of air and a hum of grav-beam generators. But I flew low over the woods and meadows, dawdling along at fifty kilometers an hour and looking across the landscape. It lay quietly in the evening, almost empty of man, a green fair breadth of land veined with bright rivers. The westering sun touched each leaf and grass blade with molten gold, an aureate glow which seemed to fill the cool air like a tangible presence, and I could hear the chirp and chatter of the great bird flocks as they settled down in the trees. Yes—it was good to get home.

My own house stood at the very edge of the sea, on a sandy bluff sloping down to the water. The windy trees which grew about it almost hid the little stone and timber structure, but its lawns and gardens reached far, and beyond them were the fields from which we got our food. Down by the beach stood the boathouse and the little dock I had made, and I knew our sailboat lay waiting there for me to take her out. I felt an almost physical hunger for the sea again, the mighty surge of waves out to the wild horizon, the keen salt wind and the crying white birds. After a month in the sterile tanked air of the spaceboat, it was like being born again.

I set the plane down before the house and got out. Two small bodies fairly exploded against me— Einar and Mike. I walked into the house with my sons riding my shoulders.

Alanna stood in the doorway waiting for me. She was tall, almost as tall as I, and slim and red-haired and the most beautiful woman in the universe. We didn't say much—it was unnecessary, and we were otherwise occupied for the next few minutes.

And afterward I sat before a leaping fire where

the little flames danced and chuckled and cast a wavering ruddy glow over the room, and the wind whistled outside and rattled the door, and the sea roared on the nighted beach, and I told them of my fabulous space voyage, which had been hard and monotonous and lonely but was a glamorous adventure at home. The boys' eyes never stirred from my face as I talked, I could feel the eagerness that blazed from them. The gaunt sun-seared crags of One, the misty jungles of Two, the mountains and deserts of Four, the great civilization of Five, the bitter desolation of the outer worlds—and beyond those the stars. But we were home now, we sat in a warm dry house and heard the wind singing outside.

I was happy, in a quiet way that had somehow lost the exuberance of my earlier returns. Content, maybe.

Oh, well, I thought. These trips to the fifth world were becoming routine, just as life on Harbor, now that our colony was established and our automatic and semiautomatic machines running smoothly, had quieted down from the first great riot of work and danger and work again. That was progress, that was what we had striven for, to remove want and woe and the knife-edged uncertainty which had haunted our days. We had arrived, we had graduated into a solid assurance and a comfort which still held enough unsureness and challenge to keep us from getting sluggish. Grown men don't risk their necks climbing the uppermost branches of trees, the way children do; they walk on the ground, and when they have to rise they do so safely and comfortably, in a carplane.

"What's the matter, Erling?" asked Alanna.

"Why—nothing." I started out of my reverie, suddenly aware that the children were in bed and the night near its middle. "Nothing at all. I was just sitting thinking. A little tired, I guess. Let's turn in."

"You're a poor liar, Erling," she said softly. "What were you really thinking about?"

"Nothing," I insisted. "That is, well, I saw the old *Traveler* as I was coming down today. It just put me in mind of old times."

"It would," she said. And suddenly she sighed. I looked at her in some alarm, but she was smiling again. "You're right, it is late, and we'd better go to bed."

I took the boys out in the sailboat the next day. Alanna stayed home on the excuse that she had to prepare dinner, though I knew of her theory that the proper psychodevelopment of children required a balance of paternal and maternal influence. Since I was away so much of the time, out in space or with one of the exploring parties which were slowly mapping our planet, she made me occupy the center of the screen whenever I was home.

Einar, who was nine years old and getting interested in the microbooks we had from the *Traveler*— and so, ultimately, from Earth—looked at her and said: "Back at Sol you wouldn't have to make food, Mother. You'd just set the au . . . autochef, and come out with us."

"I like to cook," she smiled. "I suppose we could make autochefs, now that the more important semirobot machinery has been produced, but it'd take a lot of fun out of life for me."

Her eyes went past the house, down to the beach and out over the restless sun-sparked water. The sea breeze ruffled her red hair, it was like a flame in the cool shade of the trees. "I think they must miss a lot in the Solar System," she said. "They have so much there that, somehow, they can't have what we've got—room to move about, lands that never saw a man before, the fun of making something ourselves."

"You might like it if you went there," I said. "After all, sweetheart, however wisely we may talk about Sol we know it only by hearsay."

"I know I like what we have here," she answered. I thought there was a faint note of defiance in her voice. "If Sol is just a legend, I can't be sure I'd like the reality. Certainly it could be no better than Harbor."

"All redheads are chauvinists," I laughed, turning down toward the beach.

"All Swedes make unfounded generalizations," she replied cheerfully. "I should'a known better than to marry a Thorkild."

"Fortunately, Mrs. Thorkild, you didn't." I bowed.

The boys and I got out the sailboat. There was a spanking breeze, and in minutes we were scudding northward, along the woods and fields and tumbling surf of the coast.

"We should put a motor on the *Naughty Nancy*, Dad," said Einar. "Suppose this wind don't hold."

"I like to sail," I said. "The chance of having to man the sweeps is part of the fun."

"Me too," said Mike, a little ambiguously.

"Do they have sailboats on Earth?" asked Einar.

"They must," I said, "since I designed the *Nancy* after a book about them. But I don't think it'd ever be quite the same, Einar. The sea must always be full of boats, most of them powered, and there'd be aircraft overhead and some sort of building wherever you made landfall. You wouldn't have the sea to yourself."

"Then why'd you want to keep looking for Earth when ever'body else wanted to stay here?" he challenged.

A nine-year-old can ask some remarkably disconcerting questions. I said slowly: "I wasn't the only one who voted to keep on searching. And— well, I admitted it at the time, it wasn't Earth but the search itself that I wanted. I liked to find new planets. But we've got a good home now, Einar, here on Harbor."

"I still don't understand how they ever lost Earth," he said.

"Nobody does," I said. "The *Traveler* was carrying a load of colonists to Alpha Centauri—that was a star close to Sol—and men had found the hyperdrive only a few years before and reached the nearer stars. Anyway, *something* happened. There was a great explosion in the engines, and we found ourselves somewhere else in the Galaxy, thousands of light-years from home. We don't know how far from home, since we've never been able to find Sol again. But after repairing the ship, we spent more than twenty years looking. We never found home." I added quickly, "Until we decided to settle on Harbor. That was our home."

"I mean, how'd the ship get thrown so far off?"

I shrugged. The principles of the hyperdrive are difficult enough, involving as they do the concept of multiple dimensions and of discontinuous psi functions. No one on the ship—and everyone with a knowledge of physics had twisted his brains over the problem—had been able to figure out what catastrophe it was that had annihilated space-time for her. Speculation had involved space warps—whatever that term means, points of infinite discontinuity, undimensional fields, and Cosmos knows what else. Could we find what had happened, and purposefully control the phenomenon which had seized us by some blind accident, the Galaxy would be ours. Meanwhile, we were limited to pseudo-velocities of a couple of hundred lights, and interstellar space mocked us with vastness.

But how explain that to a nine-year-old? I said only: "If I knew that, I'd be wiser than anyone else, Einar. Which I'm not."

"I wanna go swimming," said Mike.

"Sure," I said. "That was our idea, wasn't it? We'll drop anchor in the next bay—"

"I wanna go swimming in Spacecamp Cove."

I tried to hedge, but Einar was all over me, too. It was only a few kilometers farther up the coast, and its broad sheltered expanse, its wide sandy beach, and the forest immediately behind, made it ideal for such an expedition. And after all, I had nothing against it.

Nothing—except the lure of the place.

I sighed and surrendered. Spacecamp Cove it was.

We had a good time there, swimming and pic-nicking, playing ball and loafing in the sand and swimming some more. It was good to lie in the sun again, with a cool wet wind blowing in from the sea and talking in the trees. And to the boys, the glamour of it was a sort of crown on the day.

But I had to fight the romance. I wasn't a child any more, playing at spacemen and aliens, I was the grown man with some responsibilities. The community of the *Traveler* had voted by an over-whelming majority to settle on Harbor, and that was that.

And here, half hidden by long grass, half buried in the blowing sand, were the unmistakable signs of what we had left.

There wasn't much. A few plasticontainers for food, a couple of broken tools of curious shape, some scattered engine parts. Just enough to indi-cate that a while ago—ten years ago, perhaps—a party of spacemen had landed here, camped for a while, made some repairs, and resumed their journey.

They weren't from the fifth planet. Those na-tives had never left their world, and even with the technological impetus we were giving them in ex-change for their metals they weren't ever likely to, the pressures they needed to live were too great. They weren't from Sol, or even some colony world—not only were the remains totally unlike our equip-ment, but the news of a planet like Harbor, almost a duplicate of Earth but without a native intelli-gent race, would have brought settlers here in swarms. So—somewhere in the Galaxy, someone else had mastered the hyperdrive and was exploring space.

As we had been doing—

I did my best to be cheerful all the way home, and think I succeeded on the surface. And that in spite of Einar's wildly romantic gabble about the unknown campers. But I couldn't help remembering—

In twenty years of spacing, you can see a lot of worlds, and you can have a lot of experience. We had been gods of a sort, flitting from star to star, exploring, trading, learning, now and again mixing into the destinies of the natives. We had fought and striven, suffered and laughed and stood silent in wonder. For most of us, the dreadful hunger for home, the weariness of the hopeless quest, had shadowed that panorama of worlds which reeled through my mind. But—before Cosmos, I had loved every minute of it!

I fell into unrelieved moodiness as soon as we had stowed the *Naughty Nancy* in our boathouse. The boys ran ahead of me toward the house, but I followed slowly. Alanna met me at the door.

"Better wash up right away," she said. "The company will be here any minute."

"Uh-huh."

She looked at me, for a very long moment, and laid her hand on my arm. In the long dazzling rays of the westering sun, her eyes were brighter than I had seen them before. I wondered if tears were not wavering just behind them.

"You were at Spacecamp Cove," she said quietly.

"The boys wanted to go there," I answered. "It's a good place."

"Erling—" She paused. I stood looking at her, thinking how beautiful she was. I remembered the way she had looked on Hralfar, the first time I kissed her. We had wandered a ways from the camp of the detail exploring that frosty little world and negotiating with its natives for supplies. The sky had been dark overhead, with a shrunken sun casting its thin pale light on the blue-shadowed snow. It was quiet, breathlessly quiet, the air was like sharp fire in our nostrils and her hair, the only color in that white horizon, seemed to crackle with frost. That was quite a long time ago, but nothing had changed between us since.

"Yes?" I prompted her. "Yes, what is it?"

Her voice came quickly, very low so the boys wouldn't hear: "Erling, are you really happy here?"

"Why"—I felt an almost physical shock of surprise—"of course I am, dear. That's a silly question."

"Or a silly answer?" She smiled, with closed lips. "We did have some good times on the *Traveler*. Even those who grumbled loudest at the time admit that, now when they've got a little perspective on the voyage and have forgotten something of the overcrowding and danger and weariness. But you—I sometimes think the *Traveler* was your life, Erling."

"I liked the ship, of course." I had a somewhat desperate sense of defending myself. "After all, I was born and raised on her. I never really knew anything else. Our planetary visits were so short, and most of the worlds so unterrestrial. You liked it too."

"Oh, sure, it was fun to go batting around the Galaxy, never knowing what might wait at the next sun. But a woman wants a home. And—Erling, plenty of others your age, who also had never known anything else, hated it."

"I was lucky. As an officer, I had better quarters, more privacy. And, well, that 'something hid behind the ranges' maybe meant more to me than to most others. But—good Cosmos, Alanna! you don't think that now—"

"I don't think anything, Erling. But on the ship you weren't so absent-minded, so apt to fall into daydreams. You didn't sit around the place all day, you were always working on something. . . ." She bit her lip. "Don't misunderstand, Erling. I have no doubt you keep telling yourself how happy you are. You could go to your cremation, here on Harbor, thinking you'd had a rather good life. But—I sometimes wonder!"

"Now look—" I began.

"No, no, nothing more out of you. Get inside and wash up, the company'll be coming in half a minute."

I went, with my head in a whirl. Mechanically, I scrubbed myself and changed into evening blouse and slacks. When I came out of the bedroom, the first of the guests were already waiting.

MacTeague Angus was there, the old first mate of the *Traveler* and captain in the short time between Kane's death and our settling on Harbor. So was my brother Thorkild Gustav, with whom I had little in common except a mutual liking. Tokogama

Hideyoshi, Petroff Ivan, Ortega Manuel, and a couple of others showed up a few minutes later. Alanna took charge of their wives and children, and I mixed drinks all around.

For a while the talk was of local matters. We were scattered over quite a wide area, and had as yet not produced enough telescreens for every house, so that communication was limited to direct personal travel by plane. A hailstorm on Gustav's farm, a minor breakdown in the vehicle factory superintended by Ortega, Petroff's project of a fleet of semirobot fishing boats—small gossip. Presently dinner was served.

Gustav was rapturous over the steak. "What is it?" he asked.

"Some local animal I shot the other day," I said. "Ungulate, reddish-brown, broad flat horns."

"Oh, yes. Hm-m-m—I'll have to try domesticating some. I've had pretty good luck with those glug-gugs."

"Huh?" Petroff stared at him.

"Another local species," laughed Gustav. "I had to call them something, and they make that kind of noise."

"The *Traveler* was never like this," said Ortega, helping himself to another piece of meat.

"I never thought the food was bad," I said.

"No, we had the hydroponic vegetables and fruits, and the synthetic meats, as well as what we picked up on different planets," admitted Ortega. "But it wasn't this good, ever. Hydroponics somehow don't have the flavor of Earth-grown stuff."

"That's your imagination," said Petroff. "I can prove—"

"I don't care what you can prove, the facts remain." Ortega glanced at me. "But there were compensations."

"Not enough," muttered Gustav. "I've got room to move, here on Harbor."

"You're being unjust to the *Traveler*," I said. "She was only meant to carry about fifty people for a short voyage at that. When she lost her way for twenty years, and a whole new generation got jammed in with their parents, it's no wonder she grew crowded. Actually, her minimum crew is ten or so. Thirty people—fifteen couples, say, plus their kids—could travel in her in ease and comfort, with private apartments for all."

"And still . . . still, for over twenty years, we fought and suffered and stood the monotony and the hopelessness—to find Earth." Tokogama's voice was musing, a little awed. "When all the time, on any of a hundred uninhabited terrestroid planets, we could have had—this."

"For at least half that time," pointed out MacTeague, "we were simply looking for the right part of the Galaxy. We knew Sol wasn't anywhere near, so we had no hopes to be crushed, but we thought as soon as the constellations began to look fairly familiar we'd be quickly able to find home." He shrugged. "But space is simply too big, and our astrogational tables have so little information. Star travel was still in its infancy when we left Sol.

"An error of, say, one percent could throw us light-years off in the course of several hundred parsecs. And the Galaxy is lousy with GO-type suns, which are statistically almost certain to have neighbors sufficiently like Sol's to fool an unsure observer. If our tables had given positions relative to, say, S Doradus, we could have found home easily enough. But they used Sirius for their bright-star point—and we couldn't find Sirius in that swarm of stars! We just had to hop from star to star which *might* be Sol—and find it wasn't, and go on, with the sickening fear that maybe we were getting farther away all the time, maybe Sol lay just off the bows, obscured by a dark nebula. In the end—we gave it up as a bad job."

"There's more to it than that," said Tokogama. "We realized all that, you know. But there was Captain Kane and his tremendous personality, his driving will to success, and we'd all come to rely more or less blindly on him. As long as he lived, nobody quite believed in the possibility of failure. When he died, everything seemed to collapse at once."

I nodded grimly, remembering those terrible days that followed—Seymour's mutinous attempt to seize power, bringing home to us just how sick and weary we all were; the arrival at this star which might have solved it all, might have given us a happy ending, if it had been Sol; the rest on Harbor, a rest which became a permanent stay—

"Something else kept us going all those years, too," said Ortega quietly. "There was an element among the younger generation which liked to wander. The vote to stay here wasn't unanimous."

"I know," said MacTeague. His level gaze rested thoughtfully on me. "I often wonder, Erling, why some of you don't borrow the ship and visit the nearer stars, just to see what's there."

"Wouldn't do any good," I said tonelessly. "It'd just make our feet itch worse than ever—and there'd always be stars beyond those."

"But why—" Gustav fumbled for words. "Why would anyone *want* to go—stargazing that way? I . . . well, I've got my feet on ground now, my own ground, my own home . . . it's growing, I'm building and planting and seeing it come to reality before my own eyes, and it'll be there for my children and their children. There's air and wind and rain, sunlight, the sea, the woods and mountains—Cosmos! Who wants more? Who wants to trade it for sitting in a sterile metal tank, riding from star to star, homeless, hopeless?"

"Nobody," I said hastily. "I was just trying—"

"The most pointless existence—simply to be a . . . a spectator in the universe!"

"Not exactly," said Tokogama. "There was plenty we did, if you insist that somebody must do something. We brought some benefits of human civilization to quite a number of places. We did some extensive star-mapping, if we ever see Earthmen again they'll find our tables useful, and our observations within different systems. We . . . well, we were wanderers, but so what? Do you blame a bird for not having hoofs?"

"The birds have hoofs now," I said. "They're walking on the ground. And"—I flashed a glance at Alanna—"they like it."

The conversation was getting a little too hot. I steered it into safer channels until we adjourned to the living room. Over coffee and tobacco it came back.

We began reminiscing about the old days, plan-

ets we had seen, deeds we had done. Worlds and
suns and moons, whirling through a raw dark emp-
iness afire with stars, were in our talk—strange
races, foreign cities, lonely magnificence of moun-
ains and plains and seas, the giant universe open-
ng before us. Oh, by all the gods, we had fared
ar!

We had seen the blue hell-flames leaping over
he naked peaks of a planet whose great sun almost filled its sky. We had sailed with a gang of
happy pirates over a sea red as new-spilled blood
oward the grotesque towers of a fortress older
han their history. We had seen the rich color and
flashing metal of a tournament on Drangor and the
steely immensity of the continental cities on Alkan.
We had talked philosophy with a gross wallowing
cephalopod on one world and been shot at by the
inhumanly beautiful natives of another. We had
come as gods to a planet to lift its barbaric natives
from the grip of a plague that scythed them down
and we had come as humble students to the ancient laboratories and libraries of the next. We had
come near perishing in a methane storm on a planet
far from its sun and felt then how dear life is.
We had lain on the beaches of the paradise world
Luanha and let the sea sing us to sleep. We had
ridden centauroids who conversed with us as they
went to the aerial city of their winged enemies—

More than the wildly romantic adventures—
which, after all, had been pretty dirty and bloody
affairs at the time—we loved to remember the
worlds themselves: a fiery sunset on the snow-
fields of Hralfar; a great brown river flowing through
the rain forest which covered Atlang; a painted

desert on Thyvari; the mighty disk of New Jupiter swelling before our bows; the cold and vastness and cruelty and emptiness and awe and wonder of open space itself. And, in our small clique of frank tramps, there had been the comradeship of the road, the calm unspoken knowledge of having friends who would stand firm—a feeling of *belonging*, such as men like Gustav had achieved only since coming here, and which we seemed to have lost.

Lost—yes, why not admit it? We didn't see each other very often any more, we were too scattered, too busy. And the talk of the others was just a little bit boring.

Well, it couldn't be helped—

It was late that night when the party broke up, Alanna and I saw the guests out to their planes. When the last vehicle had whispered into the sky we stood for a while looking around us. The night was very still and cool, with a high starry sky in which the moon of Harbor was rising. Its light glittered on the dew under our feet, danced restlessly on the sea, threw a dim silver veil on the dreaming land—our land.

I looked down at Alanna. She was staring over the darkened view, staring as if she had never seen it before—or never would again. The moonlight was tangled like frost in her hair. *What if I never see open space again? What if I sit here till I die? This is worth it.*

She spoke at last, very slowly, as if she had to shape each word separately: "I'm beginning to realize it. Yes, I'm quite sure."

"Sure of what?" I asked.

"Don't play dumb. You know what I mean. You and Manuel and Ivan and Hideyoshi and the others who were here—except Angus and Gus, of course. And quite a few more. You don't belong here. None of you."

"How—so?"

"Look, a man who had been born and raised in a city, and had a successful life in it, couldn't be expected to take to the country all of a sudden. Maybe never. Put him among peasants, and he'd go around all the rest of his life wondering vaguely why he wasn't honestly happy."

"We— Now don't start that again, sweetheart," I begged.

"Why not? Somebody's got to. After all, Erling, this is a peasantry we've got, growing up on Harbor. More or less mechanized, to be sure, but still rooted to the soil, close to it, with the peasant strength and solidity and the peasant's provincial outlook. Why, if a ship from Earth landed tomorrow, I don't think twenty people would leave with it.

"But you, Erling, you and your friends—you grew up in the ship, and you made a successful adaptation to it. You spent your formative years wandering. By now—you're cosmopolites. For you, a mountain range will always be more than it really is, because of what's behind it. One horizon isn't enough, you've got to have many, as many as there are in the universe.

"Find Earth? Why, you yourself admitted you don't care whether Earth is ever found. You only want the search.

"You're a gypsy, Erling. And no gypsy could ever be tied to one place."

I stood for a long while, alone with her in the cold calm moonlight, and said nothing. When I looked down at her, finally, she was trying not to cry, but her lip was trembling and the tears were bright in her eyes. Every word was wrenched out of me:

"You may be right, Alanna. I'm beginning to be horribly afraid you are. But what's to be done about it?"

"Done?" She laughed, a strangely desolate laugh. "Why, it's a very simple problem. The answer is circling right there up in the sky. Get a crew who feel the way you do, and take the *Traveler*. Go roaming—forever!"

"But . . . you? You, the kids, the place here . . . you—"

"Don't you see?" Her laughter rang louder now, echoing faintly in the light night. "Don't you see? I want to go, too!" She almost fell into my arms. "I want to go, too!"

There is no reason to record the long arguments, grudging acceptances, slow preparations. In the end we won. Sixteen men and their wives, with half a dozen children, were wild to leave.

That summer blazed up into fall, winter came, spring, and summer again, while we made ready. Our last year on Harbor. And I had never realized how much I loved the planet. Almost, I gave up.

But space, free space, the open universe and the ship come alive again—!

We left the colony a complete set of plans, in

the unlikely event that they should ever want to build a starship of their own, and a couple of spaceboats and duplicates of all the important automatic machinery carried by the *Traveler*. We would make astrogating tables, as our official purpose, and theoretically we might some day come back.

But we knew we never would. We would go traveling, and our children would carry the journey on after us, and their children after them, a whole new civilization growing up between the stars, rootless but tremendously alive. Those who wearied of it could always colonize a planet; we would be spreading mankind over the Galaxy. When our descendants were many, they would build other ships until there was a fleet, a mobile city hurtling from sun to sun. It would be a culture to itself, drawing on the best which all races had to offer and spreading it over the worlds. It would be the bloodstream of the interstellar civilization which was slowly gestating in the universe.

As the days and months went by, my boys grew even more impatient to be off. I smiled a little. Right now, they only thought of the adventure of it, romantic planets and great deeds to be done. Well, there were such, they would have eventful lives, but they would soon learn that patience and steadfastness were needed, that there was toil and suffering and danger—and life!

Alanna—I was a little puzzled. She was very gay when I was around, merrier than I had ever seen her before. But she often went out for long walks, alone on the beach or in the sun-dappled woods, and she started a garden which she would never harvest. Well—so it went, and I was too busy with preparations to think much about it.

The end came, and we embarked on the long voyage, the voyage which has not ceased yet and, I hope, will never end. The night before, we had Angus and Gustav in for a farewell party, and it was a strange feeling to be saying good-by knowing that we would never see them again, or hear from them. It was like dying.

But we were alone in the morning. We went out to our carplane, to fly to the landing field where the gypsies would meet. From there, a boat would take us to the *Traveler*. I still could not fully realize that I was captain—I, captain of the great ship which had been my world, it didn't seem real. I walked slowly, my head full of the sudden universe of responsibility.

Alanna touched my arm. "Look around, Erling," she whispered. "Look around at our land. You'll never see it again."

I shook myself out of my reverie and let my eyes sweep the horizon. It was early, the grass was still wet, flashing in the new sun. The sea danced and glittered beyond the rustling trees, crying its old song to the fair green land, and the wind that blew from it was keen and cold and pungent with life. The fields were stirring in the wind, a long ripple of grass, and high overhead a bird was singing.

"It's—very beautiful," I said.

"Yes." I could hardly hear her voice. "Yes, it is. Let's go, Erling."

We got into the carplane and slanted skyward. The boys crowded forward with me, staring ahead for the first glimpse of the landing field, not seeing the forests and meadows and shining rivers that slipped away beneath us.

Alanna sat behind me, looking down over the land. Her bright head was bent away so I couldn't see her face. I wondered what she was thinking, but somehow I didn't want to ask her.

FOR THE DURATION

There were four of them. Any one of them could have broken my back in his hands, but the Ns usually worked in teams of four, and came about four in the morning. That way, they were less hampered by crowds. People by day would gather to watch an N kicking in somebody's ribs, and get in the way, but during the empty darkness before sunrise the noise of boots only made them thank Hare that they weren't receiving such guests.

As a professor at the University, I rated a single room all to my own family. After the boys grew up and Sarah died, that meant living quite alone in an eight-foot cubicle. I was therefore unpopular with everyone else in the tenement, I suspect; but my job being to think, I *needed* privacy.

"Lewisohn?" It was a word spat out, not really a

question, from the murk behind the flashbeam on my eyes.

I couldn't answer . . . my tongue was a block of wood between stiff jaws.

"It's him," grunted another voice. "Where's the gahdam switch?" He found it, and light glared from the ceiling.

I stumbled out of bed. "Get a move on, there," said the corporal. He took the bust of Nefertiti, one of the three inanimate things I loved, off the shelf and threw it at my feet. A piece of shattering plaster bruised me.

The second thing I loved, Sarah's picture, got a revolver barrel driven through it. One of the green-clad men started for the third item, my shelf of books, but the corporal halted him. "Cut it out, Joe," he said. "Doncha know the books go to Bloomington?"

"Naw. Fack?"

"Yeh. They say the Cinc collecks 'em."

Joe wrinkled his narrow forehead in puzzlement. I could follow his thoughts, in some queasy corner of my brain. Eggheads are all suspect; the Cinc is above suspicion; therefore the Cinc cannot be an egghead. But eggheads read books . . .

Actually, Hare was a complex man. I had known him slightly, many years back when he was only an ambitious junior officer. He had a wide-ranging, inquisitive mind, and was a talented amateur cellist. He was not hostile to learning *per se*—he had plenty of thinkers on his own staff—what he distrusted was the mind which went too far. His saying: "This is not a time to question it is a time to build," had become a national slogan.

"Getcha clothes on, fellow," said the corporal to me. "And pack a toothbrush—you'll be gone fr quite a while."

"Hell, he won't need no toothbrush," said another N. "No teeth by tomorrow see?" He laughed.

"Shut up. Arnold-Lewisohn-you-are-under-arrest-on-suspicion-of-violating-Section-10-of-the-Emergency-Reconstruction-Act." That was the catchall section, which had made most other laws obsolete.

At least they won't beat me here, I thought, wishing my poor skinny frame wouldn't shake so much. At least they'll wait till we get to the station. And it may take as much as half an hour to get there and book me and start beating me.

Or even longer, perhaps. Rumor had it that the Ns first quizzed a suspect under narco. If he didn't spill the beans, they concluded he must have been conditioned and turned him over to the third-degree boys. But I would reveal nothing, because I knew nothing; therefore—

"My sons . . . they—" I fumbled my tongue in my mouth. "They haven't anything to do with— Could I—"

"No letters. Get a move on!"

I groped my way into my clothes. It was very dark and quiet in the street below the window. A roadable plane whispered down the pavement. I wondered where it was bound and on what errand.

"Let's go." The nearest N helped me along with a kick.

We went down the rotting stairs and came out on the sidewalk. The night air was cold and wet in my lungs. A car waited, with the Cross-and-thunderbolt of the National Safety Corps luminous on its black flank.

The roadable plane came around the corner once more and slithered to a halt. Through hazed eyes, I saw a city police emblem on it. A man got out.

"What the hell do you want?" snapped the corporal.

Then the gas rolled over us.

I retained a wisp of consciousness. As if from very far away. I saw myself fall to the pavement. One of the Ns managed to draw his revolver and shoot before he collapsed, but his shot went wild.

A tall man stooped over me. Beneath the wide-brimmed hat, his face was inhuman with a gas mask. He got me by the arms and dragged me to the plane. There were two others with him.

We taxied down the street and purred into the sky. The light-speckled sprawl of Des Moines fell away behind us, and we rode alone under friendly stars.

It took me a while to wake up and get over the post-anesthetic wretchedness. One of the men with me handed over a bottle. It was straight rum, and helped mightily.

The tall man in the front seat turned around. "You are Professor Lewisohn, aren't you?" he inquired anxiously. "Department of Cybernetics, New American University?"

"Yes," I mumbled.

"Good." His relief whistled out between his teeth. "I was afraid we might have rescued the wrong man. Not that we wouldn't like to rescue everyone, you understand, but we could only use *you* at the Hideout. Our intelligence service isn't perfect . . . we were told you were due to be picked up tonight, but sometimes the informers slip up."

I asked, idiotically: "Why tonight? You almost didn't make it. Why not earlier?"

"Think you'd have come . . . think you'd have believed public enemies like us, you with three sons to worry about?" he answered in a dispassionate tone. "Now you've *got* to join us. The Committee will warn your boys and help them disappear, but we can't hide them forever; the N Corps is bound to smell them out in time. So your only chance of saving them, as well as yourself, is to help stage a revolution inside a month."

"Me?" I squeaked.

"Achtmann wants a cyberneticist. You'll find out."

"Say, Bill." There was a Western twang in the voice at my left. "Been wonderin'—I'm new at this game—why'd you use the gas? I could'a plugged them four goons in four seconds."

The tall man at the controls chuckled. "I prefer gas in cases like this," he said. "Those Ns are already dead men—they let an egghead be taken away from them. This way, they'll be rather more slow about dying."

The Hideout was, of all places, Virginia City, Nevada. I could remember when it was a booming tourist trap, but in this era of scarcity and restrictions, when nobody except the highest officials owned cars, it was a ghost town. A few bearded, half-crazy squatters remained, ignored by the police as harmless, shunned by the rancher and

Renoite as unconventional and therefore possible subversives.

Only . . . when those grizzled forms had tottered into the underground rooms and joined the several hundred people who never looked on the sun, their backs straightened and their voices grew crisp and they were on the Committee for the Restoration of Freedom.

It took me some days to get used to the set up. Like most folk, I had thought of the Committee as being a few scattered lunatics—like some, I had often wished it were more. And it turned out to be more, much more.

But then, it had had fifteen years in which to organize.

"We began as a bare handful," said Achtmann. "I shouldn't say 'we,' I was only thirteen at the time, but my father was one of the founders. It's grown since then, believe me, it's grown. There are almost ten million men sworn to our cause, waiting for the word. We estimate another ten million will join us when we do rise, though of course without training and organization they can't offer much except moral support."

He was a rather short young man, but lithe as a cat. His eyes were blue blowtorch flames under a wheaten shock of hair. He was never still, and he chainsmoked from his rising before dawn to his going to bed sometime after midnight.

Only the Cinc and a few others could get that many cigarets. Achtmann consumed a month's ration in a day. But the underground felt privileged to contribute to him. I did too, after the first hour.

Because Achtmann was the last hope of free men.

"Ten million people?" It seemed an impossibly large number to keep concealed. "Good Lord, how—"

"Our agents sound out various prospects . . . oh, carefully, carefully," he explained. "The likeliest ones are finally given a narco and a psych profile is taken. If they're suitable, they're in. If not—" He grimaced. "Too bad. But we can't risk some stupid innocent pouring out the whole works."

I didn't like that part of it. I wondered if Kintyre, the tall man who directed my rescue and was fond of cats and children, if he had ever put a bullet through the head of some well-intentioned, unsuitable soul. To forget, I went on with practical questions.

"But the N dragnet must pull it some of . . . our . . . people now and then," I objected. "They must find out—"

"Oh, they do. They have a pretty fair estimate of our numbers, our general system. But so what? The organization is in cells; nobody in our rank and file knows more than four other members. There are countersigns, changed at irregular short intervals—we've learned, I tell you. In fifteen years, at the price of a good many lives and setbacks, we've learned."

Then, all at once, ten million seemed a ridiculously small number. Why, there were forty million in the armed forces and the reserves alone, not counting two million Ns and—

Achtmann grinned at me when I objected. "Just let us seize Bloomington, knock off Hare and enough

Ns, and we've won. The bulk of the people are passive, they'll be too scared to act one way or another. The armed forces—well, some of them will fight, but you'd be surprised how many officers are Committee members. And in the N Corps itself—where d'you think we get all our information?" His finger stabbed at me, he spoke with his usual feverish haste. "Look, for a long time now, ever since World War II, mediocrity has been on the march. World War III and the Hare dictatorship have simply given mediocrity a gun and a club to enforce itself. Isn't that going to gall every able-minded man in the world? Didn't he chafe you? So the intelligent, inquiring people will tend to drift into our cause—we smuggle some of 'em back into the enemy's camp—and because of being able, they soon rise high in the enemy's ranks!"

He stubbed out his cigaret and prowled about the cluttered, dusty office. "I'll agree, ten million men, loosely organized, without an H-bomb to their name, can't overthrow a planet-wide empire as things are now. But you see, Lewisohn, we aren't just going to pit submachine guns against tanks. We're going to be equipped with a weapon that will make the tanks and bombs obsolete, worse than useless! And that's where you come in."

Let it be clearly understood, Hare was not a dog unleashed from hell. He was a strong, intelligent, not unkindly man who wrought enormous good. Don't forget, it was his work that the East and West coasts are again inhabited. Even though the radioactivity was gone, people were afraid to move back. He forced them back, gave them plows in their hands and earthworms in their soil, and regained a quarter of the continent.

I think, now, that Hare or someone like him was inevitable. After World War III, if you can call a few days of nuclear butchery followed by several years of starvation and chaos a war, the world power which is safety waited for the first country to become civilized again. Hare, an obscure brigadier, used his tattered command as a starting point. People came to him because he offered food and hope. So did other war lords, but Hare whipped them. Hare also whipped China and Egypt, when they made their own tries at supremacy, and turned all Earth into the Protectorate.

Yes, he was a dictator. But nothing else was possible. I had supported him myself, even fought in his army two decades ago. We needed a Cincinnatus—then.

"For the duration of the emergency," read the Act of Congress. There was a handpicked Congress in Bloomington, and a frightened little shadow of a President, and a rubber-stamp Supreme Court. Under the law, Hare was only Commander-in-Chief of the National Safety Corps, an executive arm in the Department of Defense & Justice. His nominal superior was appointed by the President and confirmed by the Senate. He had retired from the Army to "maintain civilian control of government."

However, for the duration of the emergency the Cinc possessed extraordinary powers. And now we had rebuilt a great deal, and the world—if not quiet or content—was safely under guard, and one might think the emergency was past.

Only somehow . . . well, there was the mutant typhus epidemic, and next year there was an uprising in Indonesia, and next year the Colorado Valley Authority needed five million laborers, and next year there was a big scare about subversives, and so it went for twenty years.

Somehow, Cincinnatus never had gone back to his plow.

I didn't know the details of Committee organization. I didn't care to, wasn't allowed to, and didn't have time to. Let it merely be said that this was as carefully planned a coup as history has ever seen.

Not yet thirty, Achtmann *was* the revolution. Of course, he didn't handle all the details—he had staffs for the military, economic, and political aspects. But he kept his finger on everything, the flow of memos from his desk was incredible, and it was to him we all turned in our need.

Things just happened to work out that way. Achtmann's father had been the guiding genius of the early days, and the son had grown up at the father's side. When the old man was found dead over his desk one morning, and the young man had naturally been called on for advice—nobody else knew as much of all the ramifications—and suddenly, two years later, the Board of Directors realized that they hadn't yet elected a new president and unanimously called on the boy-wonder.

The force shield was Achtmann's baby. His unappeasable reading appetite turned up an obscure article in a physics journal, published just before the war broke out, concerning an anomalous effect observed when an electric field of a certain high strength pulsated in a certain complex pattern of high frequencies. Achtmann called in one of his tame physicists, asked him what equipment would be needed, and had the equipment stolen piecemeal and smuggled to the Hideout. After two years of work, the possibility of a force shield became clear. In the next five years, the engineering details were hammered forth. A year later, a screen generator tested out successfully. Now, two years afterward, the parts were ready for assembly.

We didn't have the facilities to machine every part into identity. Therefore each unit had to be separately phased in, a delicate operation requiring a high-speed computer plugged into the generator circuit. I was there to serve the computer.

I forgot about sleeping, almost, for the next three weeks. It was freedom I worked for, and my sons where they huddled in fear, and the memory of old Professor Biancini. The Ns might have found it necessary to string Biancini to a lamp post, but soaking him with gasoline and igniting him had been pure, pointless enthusiasm. . . .

Achtmann looked at me across the desk. His broad square face was very white, he was one of those who never dared go above ground. "Coffee?" he asked. "It's mostly chicory, but it's at least warm and wet."

"Thanks," I said.

"And you're really all done." His hand shook a little as he poured for me. "It seems hard to believe."

"The last unit was mounted and tested an hour ago," I said. "The trucks are already on their way."

"D-day." His eyes were empty, staring at the clock on the wall. "In forty-eight hours, then."

Suddenly he lowered his face into his hands. "What am I going to do?" he whispered.

I blinked at him. "Why . . . lead the revolution . . . aren't you?" I said after a long stillness.

"Oh, yes. Yes. But after that?" He leaned over the desk, shivering. "I like you, Professor. You're very like my father, did you know that? Only a more kindly man. My father was nothing but Revolution, the great holy cause. Can you imagine growing up under a man who was not a man but a disembodied will? Can you imagine never once, in fifteen years of youth and young manhood, never once laying down the load to have a glass of beer with your friends, kissing a girl, hearing a concert, steering a sailboat over blue water? I was seventeen years old when a young couple on a day's outing blundered into Virginia City and saw too much—I ordered them shot—me, seventeen years old." His face sank back into his hands. "A lot of decent people are going to die in the next week or so . . . not just on our side. My God, do you think after ordering that I can retire to—to—what am I *able* to become?"

It grew very quiet, below his heavy breathing.

"Get out," he said finally, not looking at me. "Report to General Thomas, logistics office. You'll be needed. We'll all be needed."

As civilians—on trains, buses, planes, trucks, from the whole continent, from scattered posts of empire around the planet—our army closed in on Bloomington. The movement was not caught by the usual traffic analysis, because a carefully engineered revolt had begun in Mexico. It was a revolt doomed and damned from the start, a diversion where ragged peons met flamethrowers, but such are the necessities of war.

At various points, small towns, farms, weed-grown fields not yet resettled, our units formed themselves and moved against the Capitol.

I am not a tactician, and I still don't know the details. My department was only the force screens. Each unit was centered around a heavy truck carrying a micropile to power a shield generator. Overhead went our aircraft, ridiculous little cubjets and limping machines salvaged from junk-heaps . . . but in every squadron, one ship bore a generator.

The screen, when created, is only visible through a faint glow of ionization, as a sphere up to half a mile across. It permeates solid matter without noticeable effect. But it is a force of the same order as that which binds atomic nuclei together. And it forbids velocities above a few feet per second. A particle which travels faster and encounters the field is stopped cold, its energy of motion converted into heat.

So bullets, shells, shrapnel melt and fall to the ground. The detonation of a bomb, nuclear or chemical, involves high-speed molecules or electrons in the arming mechanism, so a bomb will not explode within the field. Radioactive dust and gas disintegrate as usual, but the energetic fragments which would normally kill a man emerge as harm-

less ions. Chemical toxins remain effective, bu
are easily guarded against.

We had machine guns and light artillery elec
tronically coupled to the screen generators. At the
moment of firing, the screens went off for the few
milliseconds needed to pass through a burst aimec
at the enemy.

The N Corps had armored vehicles. They lurched
huge and threatening, up into the field; and thei
motors stopped and their guns wouldn't shoot
Our troops would plant a magnetic mine next te
such a tank and continue. As soon as their prog
ress carried the field beyond the stalled vehicle
the mine went off.

The screens were carefully heterodyned; they
did not affect the motors of our own army, or the
various cybernetic controls. We did use some rathe
primitive methods of communication, though, since
field telephones and radio were nullified.

Destroying without being destroyed, we slugged
our way into Bloomington. A thousand planes were
called, and broke themselves against our impervi
ous little air force. We commanded land and sky
and could not be stopped.

But it was a slow and brutal way to travel. The
Ns and some Army units blocked us with shee
mass. We trampled them down, and men with
bayonets rose to meet us inside our own screens
and we ran them down with tanks. A small atomi
bomb exploded just outside the shield of our for
ward unit. Its gases and ions didn't get through
but the fireball light blinded some men, the infra
red cooked others, the gamma radiation condemnec
a few to a long dying.

The bomb also removed several residential blocks, since by that time we had entered the city. Thereafter the enemy had to contend with mass panic.

Elsewhere in the nation, TV stations were seized and the film record of Achtmann played over and over. He was not a good speaker, but perhaps that only underlined the sincerity of what he told the world, that he had come to deliver men from slavery.

I rode in a jeep with Kintyre—maintenance division—as the inevitable shocks and accidents caused our generators to misbehave. It was bitterly cold inside the field, which strained out all the warm-air molecules. Afterward you could trace our course by the sere grass and trees autumnal in midsummer. Racing from unit to unit, over smashed homes and ripped corpses, shell-pocked streets and disputed basements. I went from winter to summer and back again, and it seemed curious that we, in our springtime of hope, should bring this cold.

We bumped up to the Capitol through twilight. It was burning. A sentry passed us, and we entered the grounds. Our tires bit into lawns and flattened rosebeds. The familiar shield van was parked massive in the backyard, etched against the roar of heat and flame.

"It just quit on us," said the man with the colonel's brassard over sooty working clothes. "We want to put out this damn fire—hell, the records're in there, maybe Hare himself. The screen'll stop the fire, but we can't get a flicker out of the generator."

I called for a lantern and went to look into the van. When I plugged in my testing unit, the problem was clear enough, the soldered connection of Tube 36 had broken loose. "Easy to fix," I grumbled in my weariness, "but I'm getting tired of it. All day it's been nothing but Tube 36 here, Tube 36 there."

"That's one of the bugs we can iron out later," said Kintyre.

"Later?" I began unscrewing the main plate. "Does there have to be a later? I thought—"

"Lot of holdouts, all over the world," said Kintyre. "Maybe you know more about it, Colonel, but I think we'll have a lot of stubborn little N fortresses to squelch."

"Oh, yes." The officer looked away from the flames. "Just got word there's an armored brigade on its way. It'll be here before sunrise, and we'll have to be ready to meet it."

"We seem to hold the city, though," drawled Kintyre. "What's left of it."

"I suppose we do. Messy business. Never thought it'd be this messy. But I'm only a general superintendent in a cannery. Heck of a note, ain't it, taking a cannery superintendent and slapping a brassard on him and calling him Colonel?"

I pulled away the faceplate and joined the broken connection and called for my soldering iron. A man handed it to me. He had a rifle in his other hand, and there was a smear of blood across his face.

"Wonder if old Hare got away," said Kintyre.

"Doubt it," said the colonel. "Not a plane o theirs got off the ground here. He's probably roast ing right in this house. He had his own apartment in the Capitol, you know." He shifted on his feet and groped for a cigaret. "Damn it to hell," he said querulously, "we've got the lousiest QM in history. I ordered coffee half an hour ago."

I got the generator going. The temperature skidded down toward freezing and the flames went out as if a giant had snuffed them. Under the glare of headlights, men moved forward to probe the ruins.

"We'd better get back," said Kintyre to me.

"Wait a bit," I requested. "I'd like to know what became of Hare. He murdered quite a few good friends of mine."

The body was in the west wing apartment. It was not so burned as to be unrecognizable. He had shot his wife, to save her from the fire, but had met it himself.

The colonel looked away, sickly. "Wish they'd hurry up that coffee," he said. "All right, Sergeant, take a squad and put this thing up in front of the gates."

"What?" I asked.

"Achtmann's orders. He says we can't have a story growing up about Hare not being dead after all."

"Grisly thing to do," I said.

"Yeh," said the colonel. "But this is an emergency, you know, and we'll all have to do a lot of things we'd rather not, for the duration. Sergeant . . . no, he's busy . . . you there, Corporal, go find out what the hell became of that coffee."

I met my sons one by one, as they came out of hiding in response to the broadcasts. I could have kissed Achtmann's feet.

Then I returned to the University. I had my old room back, though so much housing had been destroyed in the revolution that I had to double up with another man.

The President had been killed by a stray bomb at Bloomington . . . poor little guy, nobody hated him. The Vice President and Cabinet had been strong Hare men. So Achtmann appointed a new executive branch. He himself refused all offices, and spent a month or so touring the country and recieving all the honors he could be given; then he returned to the capital. An election was to be held next year when things had quieted down.

In the meantime, of course, it was necessary to stamp out the remaining N bands, and the new Federal police had to be granted special powers if they were to track down all the Hareists hidden among ordinary folk. Some units of the Army attempted a counter-revolution and were suppressed. A crop failure in China required that a great deal of rice be requisitioned from Burma, which touched off a small but bloody war with the Burmese nationalists.

I hated to think of that. I had hoped we would get off the sorry road of empire and return to the rest of the world its freedom. A new party, the Libertarian, was being formed to run a slate for national office; its chief plank was the abolition of the Protectorate. I helped organize it locally. Our opponents were the more conservative Federationists. The government in Bloomington was nonpartisan, a steering committee for the duration only; but of course it could not sit on its hands, it had to take some kind of positive action in every emergency. And we had an emergency every day, it seemed.

In December the A.A.A.S. held a convention in Bloomington and I went, mostly to get away from the roommate assigned to me. We didn't like each other much.

I left the barracks and walked out into the grimy slush of winter streets. A few tattered Christmas decorations had been strung up, but there was no real sales campaign—there was no merchandise to speak of. However, the day before there had been a colorful military parade.

I walked under a low leaden sky, huddled into my overcoat. There weren't many people around, and none of them looked very cheerful. Well, that was understandable, with half the city still charred wreckage. But I missed the Salvation Army and their Christmas carols. Hare had done away with them years ago, on the grounds that private charity was too inefficient, and the new government had apparently not gotten around to rescinding his edict. The Salvation Army people had played badly and gallantly on winter corners when I was young, and it would have been pleasant to have them back.

I passed the Capitol. A new one was rising on the ruins of the old. It was supposed to be a very ornate and beautiful structure, which sounded odd when people were living in tarpaper shacks, but there was still only a steel skeleton, cold against the sky.

I wasn't going any special place. There were no meetings this afternoon which interested me. I only felt like walking. It was a shock when two large men grabbed my arms.

"Where you think you're going?"

I blinked. There was a high stone wall enclosing a large house on my left. "No place," I said. "Just out for a walk."

"Yeah? Let's see your ID."

I showed it to them. A car went past us, through the gates, with a bristling escort of armed men in gray uniforms. Maybe the new President lived here. I hadn't seen a newscast in weeks, too busy.

Hands patted me, feeling for weapons. "I guess he's okay," said one of the men.

"Yeah. On your way, Lewisohn, and don't come through this block again. Restricted. Didn't you see the signs?"

A man in peacock livery came running out of the gate. "Hey, there!" he called, "Stop!"

We halted. The man bowed to me. "Are you Professor Lewisohn, sir?" he asked. I nodded. "Then please come with me." I couldn't resist a smug grin at the Secret Service boys.

We went up a landscaped driveway and through a door. There were sentries on the porch, but inside, it was all butlers and luxury. At the end of a paneled corridor was a long room with a broad picture window overlooking a glass-roofed garden, tropical in midwinter.

The man who stood there turned around as I entered. "Prof!" he said delightedly. "Come in, for heaven's sake. Have a drink."

It was Achtmann, colorful in lounging pajamas but still the same chainsmoking, unrestful Achtmann. He took my coat and handed it to a servant.

Another servant materialized with Scotch on the rocks. I found myself in an armchair, with Achtmann pacing up and down before me.

"Good Lord," he said. "I had no idea you were in town, old fellow. If I hadn't happened to see you from my car . . . Why didn't you let me know? My secretaries have a list of Committee members, and any letter from one of them goes directly to me."

"I . . . out of touch—" I sipped carefully, seeking balance. "Busy and well, under present conditions I've sort of lost contact and—"

"What conditions?" His eyes stabbed at me. "Anything wrong?"

"Oh, no, no. Tight housing, tight schedule, the usual."

"Like hell it's usual. Not for anybody who did what you did." Achtmann whirled on a dictograph. "I can guess your troubles—lousy little room, lousy commoner's ration, lousy pay . . . eh? Okay, we'll fix it." He rattled an order into the tube: effective immediately, Professor Lewisohn was to have a house at his disposal, funds equivalent to, etc., ration-free ID, etc., etc. "Why didn't you let me know?" he finished. "I've set up all the other boys from the old Hideout gang, or most of them."

"But I don't want—" I stammered. "I don't deserve—don't throw somebody out of their house just to—"

"Shut up," he laughed. It was a boy's laugh, but there was a metal note behind it. "Quite apart from gratitude and solidarity and all that sort of thing, it's sound policy, and I won't hear no from you. The populace at large need the carrot as well as the stick. They've not only got to realize that the disloyal are punished, but see how the loyal get rewarded. Savvy?"

"What the hell kind of office do you have?" I whispered.

"Office? Position? None whatsoever. That's the beauty of it. I'm just an unofficial adviser to the President." Achtmann shrugged, wryly. "*Primus inter pares*. Somebody has to be, you realize, and I have a large following of trained men personally loyal to me, which is a big help, and this job . . . oh, call it leadership . . . is all I was ever trained for. It works out pretty well, don't you think?"

"For you it does," I said thinly.

"Hell! You think I want a hundred nosy servants under my roof? It's just part of the show I have to put on. It was Hare's mistake, being so drably correct he never gave anyone a vicarious thrill. You can't steer an entire world out of ruin without giving it a Leader in great big capital letters."

"I thought that was what you fought against," I whispered.

"It was. It still is. Of course! Only there's so much to do. We can't turn over the reins in a week to people who for a generation haven't been allowed to do their own thinking. We can't reinstate search warrants, and habeas corpus, and due process in political trials, when several million men are plotting and jockeying to restore the dictatorship. There are still a lot of devout Hareists, you know, not to mention a hundred little lunatic groups, with their own exclusive schemes for saving mankind." Achtmann lit another cigaret from the stub in his mouth.

Words, cold as ice, rattled out of him. "We can't dissolve the Protectorate and turn the foreign provinces loose, not till they've been educated and civilized, or there'll soon be another atomic war to fight. And here at home, there's so much poverty and hunger . . . how interested do you think a man is in democratic government when his children don't have bread? If we allowed it, he'd follow the first tinpot, crackpot Fuehrer who promised to feed him. We've got to restore the economy, the—"

I surprised myself by interrupting him. "For your information," I said, "I'm in the Libertarian Party."

"No matter," answered Achtmann cheerfully. "It won't be held against you. When the political parties are dissolved, it'll simply be a question of—"

"*Dissolved!*" I choked. "But there was to be an election—"

"I'm afraid it'll have to wait a few years. Honestly, old fellow, how do you think we could hold an election with conditions what they are? I thought we could, that's why it was announced, but since then I've picked up enough facts to show me I was wrong." Achtmann chuckled. "Don't look so horrified. I'm not another Hare. *He* never admitted he could be mistaken."

"You don't have to," I mumbled. "You have no title . . . the President and Congress front for you, take the blame for your errors and excesses, and you get all the credit for whatever goes right. Oh, yes."

"Ridiculous!" For a moment he was angry. Then

he turned his back on me and stared out the window.

As if on some hidden signal, the butler cat-footed in and held my coat for me. I stood up, shakily, and began putting it on.

"Don't worry, Professor," said Achtmann in a mild voice. "All right, if you insist, this is a dictatorship. But it's a benevolent one—hell, you know me and what I stand for, don't you? We may have to kill a few here and there, and people in this town are beginning to call me the Cinc, but—" He still didn't face me:

"It's only for the duration of the emergency."

DUEL ON SYRTIS

The night whispered the message. Over the many miles of loneliness it was borne, carried on the wind, rustled by the half-sentient lichens and the dwarfed trees, murmured from one to another of the little creatures that huddled under crags, in caves, by shadowy dunes. In no words, but in a dim pulsing of dread which echoed through Kreega's brain, the warning ran—

They are hunting again.

Kreega shuddered in a sudden blast of wind. The night was enormous around him, above him, from the iron bitterness of the hills to the wheeling, glittering constellations light-years over his head. He reached out with his trembling perceptions, tuning himself to the brush and the wind and the small burrowing things underfoot, letting the night speak to him.

Alone, alone. There was not another Martian for a hundred miles of emptiness. There were only the tiny animals and the shivering brush and the thin, sad blowing of the wind.

The voiceless scream of dying traveled through the brush, from plant to plant, echoed by the fear-pulses of the animals and the ringingly reflecting cliffs. They were curling, shriveling and blackening as the rocket poured the glowing death down on them, and the withering veins and nerves cried to the stars.

Kreega huddled against a tall gaunt crag. His eyes were like yellow moons in the darkness, cold with terror and hate and a slowly gathering resolution. Grimly, he estimated that the death was being sprayed in a circle some ten miles across. And he was trapped in it, and soon the hunter would come after him.

He looked up to the indifferent glitter of stars, and a shudder went along his body. Then he sat down and began to think.

It had started a few days before, in the private office of the trader Wisby.

"I came to Mars," said Riordan, "to get me an owlie."

Wisby had learned the value of a poker face. He peered across the rim of his glass at the other man, estimating him.

Even in God-forsaken holes like Port Armstrong one had heard of Riordan. Heir to a million-dollar shipping firm which he himself had pyramided into a System-wide monster, he was equally well known as a big game hunter. From the firedrakes of Mercury to the ice crawlers of Pluto, he'd bagged them all. Except, of course, a Martian. That particular game was forbidden now.

He sprawled in his chair, big and strong and ruthless, still a young man. He dwarfed the unkempt room with his size and the hard-held dynamo strength in him, and his cold green gaze dominated the trader.

"It's illegal, you know," said Wisby. "It's a twenty-year sentence if you're caught at it."

"Bah! The Martian Commissioner is at Ares, halfway round the planet. If we go at it right, who's ever to know?" Riordan gulped at his drink. "I'm well aware that in another year or so they'll have tightened up enough to make it impossible. This is the last chance for any man to get an owlie. That's why I'm here."

Wisby hesitated, looking out the window. Port Armstrong was no more than a dusty huddle of domes, interconnected by tunnels, in a red waste of sand stretching to the near horizon. An Earthman in airsuit and transparent helmet was walking down the street and a couple of Martians were lounging against a wall. Otherwise nothing—a silent, deadly monotony brooding under the shrunken sun. Life on Mars was not especially pleasant for a human.

"You're not falling into this owlie-loving that's corrupted all Earth?" demanded Riordan contemptuously.

"Oh, no," said Wisby. "I keep them in their place around my post. But times are changing. It can't be helped."

"There was a time when they were slaves," said

Riordan. "Now those old women on Earth want to give 'em the vote." He snorted.

"Well, times are changing," repeated Wisby mildly. "When the first humans landed on Mars a hundred years ago, Earth had just gone through the Hemispheric Wars. The worst wars man had ever known. They damned near wrecked the old ideas of liberty and equality. People were suspicious and tough—they'd had to be, to survive. They weren't able to—to empathize the Martians, or whatever you call it. Not able to think of them as anything but intelligent animals. And Martians made such useful slaves—they need so little food or heat or oxygen, they can even live fifteen minutes or so without breathing at all. And the wild Martians made fine sport—intelligent game, that could get away as often as not, or even manage to kill the hunter."

"I know," said Riordan. "That's why I want to hunt one. It's no fun if the game doesn't have a chance."

"It's different now," went on Wisby. "Earth has been at peace for a long time. The liberals have gotten the upper hand. Naturally, one of their first reforms was to end Martian slavery."

Riordan swore. The forced repatriation of Martians working on his spaceships had cost him plenty. "I haven't time for your philosophizing," he said. "If you can arrange for me to get a Martian, I'll make it worth your while."

"How much worth it?" asked Wisby.

They haggled for a while before settling on a figure. Riordan had brought guns and a small rocketboat, but Wisby would have to supply radioactive material, a "hawk," and a rockhound. Then he had to be paid for the risk of legal action, though that was small. The final price came high.

"Now, where do I get my Martian?" inquired Riordan. He gestured at the two in the street. "Catch one of them and release him in the desert?"

It was Wisby's turn to be contemptuous. "One of them? Hah! Town loungers! A city dweller from Earth would give you a better fight."

The Martians didn't look impressive. They stood only some four feet high on skinny, claw-footed legs, and the arms, ending in bony four-fingered hands, were stringy. The chests were broad and deep, but the waists were ridiculously narrow. They were viviparous, warm-blooded, and suckled their young, but gray feathers covered their hides. The round, hook-beaked heads, huge amber eyes and tufted feather ears, showed the origin of the name "owlie." They wore only pouched belts and carried sheath knives; even the liberals of Earth weren't ready to allow the natives modern tools and weapons. There were too many old grudges.

"The Martians always were good fighters," said Riordan. "They wiped out quite a few Earth settlements in the old days."

"The wild ones," agreed Wisby. "But not these. They're just stupid laborers, as dependent on our civilization as we are. You want a real old timer, and I know where one's to be found."

He spread a map on the desk. "See, here in the Hraefnian Hills, about a hundred miles from here. These Martians live a long time, maybe two centuries, and this fellow Kreega has been around since the first Earthmen came. He led a lot of Martian raids in the early days, but since the general amnesty and peace he's lived all alone up there, in one of the old ruined towers. A real old-time warrior who hates Earthmen's guts. He comes here once in a while with furs and minerals to trade, so I know a little about him." Wisby's eyes gleamed savagely. "You'll be doing us all a favor by shooting the arrogant bastard. He struts around here as if the place belonged to him. And he'll give you a run for your money."

Riordan's massive dark head nodded in satisfaction.

The man had a bird and a rockhound. That was bad. Without them, Kreega could lose himself in the labyrinth of caves and canyons and scrubby thickets—but the hound could follow his scent and the bird could spot him from above.

To make matters worse, the man had landed near Kreega's tower. The weapons were all there—now he was cut off, unarmed and alone save for what feeble help the desert life could give. Unless he could double back to the place somehow—but meanwhile he had to survive.

He sat in a cave, looking down past a tortured wilderness of sand and bush and wind-carved rock, miles in the thin clear air to the glitter of metal where the rocket lay. The man was a tiny speck in the huge barren landscape, a lonely insect crawling under the deep-blue sky. Even by day, the stars glistened in the tenuous atmosphere. Weak pallid sunlight spilled over rocks tawny and ocherous and rust-red, over the low dusty thorn-bushes and the gnarled little trees and the sand that blew faintly between them. Equatorial Mars!

Lonely or not, the man had a gun that could

spang death clear to the horizon, and he had his beasts, and there would be a radio in the rocketboat for calling his fellows. And the glowing death ringed them in, a charmed circle which Kreega could not cross without bringing a worse death on himself than the rifle would give—

Or was there a worse death than that—to be shot by a monster and have his stuffed hide carried back as a trophy for fools to gape at? The old iron pride of his race rose in Kreega, hard and bitter and unrelenting. He didn't ask much of life these days—solitude in his tower to think the long thoughts of a Martian, and create the small exquisite artworks which he loved; the company of his kind at the Gathering Season, grave ancient ceremony and acrid merriment and the chance to beget and rear sons; an occasional trip to the Earthling settlement for the metal goods and the wine which were the only valuable things they had brought to Mars; a vague dream of raising his folk to a place where they could stand as equals before all the universe. No more. And now they would take even this from him!

He rasped a curse on the human and resumed his patient work, chipping a spearhead for what puny help it could give him. The brush rustled dryly in alarm, tiny hidden animals squeaked their terror, the desert shouted to him of the monster that strode towards his cave. But he didn't have to flee right away.

Riordan sprayed the heavy-metal isotope in a ten-mile circle around the old tower. He did that by night, just in case patrol craft might be snooping around. But once he had landed, he was safe—he could always claim to be peacefully exploring, hunting leapers or some such thing.

The radioactive had a half-life of about four days, which meant that it would be unsafe to approach for some three weeks—two at a minimum. That was time enough, when the Martian was boxed in so small an area.

There was no danger that he would try to cross it. The owlies had learned what radioactivity meant, back when they fought the humans. And their vision, extending well into the ultra-violet, made it directly visible to them through its fluorescence to say nothing of the wholly unhuman extra senses they had. No, Kreega would try to hide, and perhaps to fight, and eventually he'd be cornered.

Still, there was no use taking chances. Riordan set a timer on the boat's radio. If he didn't come back within two weeks to turn it off, it would emit a signal which Wisby would hear, and he'd be rescued.

He checked his other equipment. He had an airsuit designed for Martian conditions, with a small pump operated by a powerbeam from the boat to compress the atmosphere sufficiently for him to breathe it. The same unit recovered enough water from his breath so that the weight of supplies for several days was, in Martian gravity, not too great for him to bear. He had a .45 rifle built to shoot in Martian air, that was heavy enough for his purposes. And, of course, compass and binoculars and sleeping bag. Pretty light equipment, but he preferred a minimum anyway.

For ultimate emergencies there was the little

tank of suspensine. By turning a valve, he could release it into his air system. The gas didn't exactly induce suspended animation, but it paralyzed efferent nerves and slowed the overall metabolism to a point where a man could live for weeks on one lungful of air. It was useful in surgery, and had saved the life of more than one interplanetary explorer whose oxygen system went awry. But Riordan didn't expect to have to use it. He certainly hoped he wouldn't. It would be tedious to lie fully conscious for days waiting for the automatic signal to call Wisby.

He stepped out of the boat and locked it. No danger that the owlie would break in if he should double back; it would take tordenite to crack that hull.

He whistled to his animals. They were native beasts, long ago domesticated by the Martians and later by man. The rockhound was like a gaunt wolf, but huge-breasted and feathered, a tracker as good as any Terrestrial bloodhound. The "hawk" had less resemblance to its counterpart of Earth; it was a bird of prey, but in the tenuous atmosphere it needed a six-foot wingspread to lift its small body. Riordan was pleased with their training.

The hound bayed, a low quavering note which would have been muffled almost to inaudibility by the thin air and the man's plastic helmet had the suit not included microphones and amplifiers. It circled, sniffing, while the hawk rose into the alien sky.

Riordan did not look closely at the tower. It was a crumbling stump atop a rusty hill, unhuman and grotesque. Once, perhaps ten thousand years ago, the Martians had had a civilization of sorts, cities and agriculture and a neolithic technology. But according to their own traditions they had achieved a union or symbiosis with the wild life of the planet and had abandoned such mechanical aids as unnecessary. Riordan snorted.

The hound bayed again. The noise seemed to hang eerily in the still, cold air; to shiver from cliff and crag and die reluctantly under the enormous silence. But it was a bugle call, a haughty challenge to a world grown old—stand aside, make way, here comes the conqueror!

The animal suddenly loped forward. He had a scent. Riordan swung into a long, easy low-gravity stride. His eyes gleamed like green ice. The hunt was begun!

Breath sobbed in Kreega's lungs, hard and quick and raw. His legs felt weak and heavy, and the thudding of his heart seemed to shake his whole body.

Still he ran, while the frightful clamor rose behind him and the padding of feet grew ever nearer. Leaping, twisting, bounding from crag to crag, sliding down shaly ravines, and slipping through clumps of trees, Kreega fled.

The hound was behind him and the hawk soaring overhead. In a day and a night they had driven him to this, running like a crazed leaper with death baying at his heels—he had not imagined a human could move so fast or with such endurance.

The desert fought for him; the plants with their queer blind life that no Earthling would ever understand were on his side. Their thorny branches twisted away as he darted through and then came

back to rake the flanks of the hound, slow him—
but they could not stop his brutal rush. He ripped
past their strengthless clutching fingers and yam-
mered on the trail of the Martian.

The human was toiling a good mile behind, but
showed no sign of tiring. Still Kreega ran. He had
to reach the cliff edge before the hunter saw him
through his rifle sights—had to, had to, and the
hound was snarling a yard behind now.

Up the long slope he went. The hawk fluttered,
striking at him, seeking to lay beak and talons in
his head. He batted at the creature with his spear
and dodged around a tree. The tree snaked out a
branch from which the hound rebounded, yelling
till the rocks rang.

The Martian burst onto the edge of the cliff. It
fell sheer to the canyon floor, five hundred feet of
iron-streaked rock tumbling into windy depths.
Beyond, the lowering sun glared in his eyes. He
paused only an instant, etched black against the
sky, a perfect shot if the human should come into
view, and then he sprang over the edge.

He had hoped the rockhound would go shooting
past, but the animal braked itself barely in time,
Kreega went down the cliff face, clawing into every tiny crevice, shuddering as the age-worn rock
crumbled under his fingers. The hawk swept close,
hacking at him and screaming for its master. He
couldn't fight it, not with every finger and toe
needed to hang against shattering death, but—

He slid along the face of the precipice into a
gray-green clump of vines, and his nerves thrilled
forth the appeal of the ancient symbiosis. The
hawk swooped again and he lay unmoving, rigid as

if dead, until it cried in shrill triumph and settled on his shoulder to pluck out his eyes.

Then the vines stirred. They weren't strong, but their thorns sank into the flesh and it couldn't pull loose. Kreega toiled on down into the canyon while the vines pulled the hawk apart.

Riordan loomed hugely against the darkening sky. He fired, once, twice, the bullets humming wickedly close, but as shadows swept up from the depths the Martian was covered.

The man turned up his speech amplifier and his voice rolled and boomed monstrously through the gathering night, thunder such as dry Mars had not heard for millennia: "Score one for you! But it isn't enough! I'll find you!"

The sun slipped below the horizon and night came down like a falling curtain. Through the darkness Kreega heard the man laughing. The old rocks trembled with his laughter.

Riordan was tired with the long chase and the niggling insufficiency of his oxygen supply. He wanted a smoke and hot food, and neither was to be had. Oh, well, he'd appreciate the luxuries of life all the more when he got home—with the Martian's skin.

He grinned as he made camp. The little fellow was a worthwhile quarry, that was for damn sure. He'd held out for two days now, in a little ten-mile circle of ground, and he'd even killed the hawk. But Riordan was close enough to him now so that the hound could follow his spoor, for Mars had no watercourses to break a trail. So it didn't matter.

He lay watching the splendid night of stars. It would get cold before long, unmercifully cold, but his sleeping bag was a good-enough insulator to keep him warm with the help of solar energy stored during the day by its Gergen cells. Mars was dark at night, its moons of little help—Phobos a hurtling speck, Deimos merely a bright star. Dark and cold and empty. The rockhound had burrowed into the loose sand nearby, but it would raise the alarm if the Martian should come sneaking near the camp. Not that that was likely—he'd have to find shelter somewhere too, if he didn't want to freeze.

The bushes and the trees and the little furtive animals whispered a word he could not hear, chattered and gossiped on the wind about the Martian who kept himself warm with work. But he didn't understand that language which was no language.

Drowsily, Riordan thought of past hunts. The big game of Earth, lion and tiger and elephant and buffalo and sheep on the high sun-blazing peaks of the Rockies. Rain forests of Venus and the coughing roar of a many-legged swamp monster crashing through the trees to the place where he stood waiting. Primitive throb of drums in a hot wet night, chant of beaters dancing around a fire— scramble along the hellplains of Mercury with a swollen sun licking against his puny insulating suit— the grandeur and desolation of Neptune's liquid-gas swamps and the huge blind thing that screamed and blundered after him—

But this was the loneliest and strangest and perhaps most dangerous hunt of all, and on that account the best. He had no malice toward the Martian; he respected the little being's courage as he respected the bravery of the other animals he had fought. Whatever trophy he brought home from this chase would be well earned.

The fact that his success would have to be treated discreetly didn't matter. He hunted less for the glory of it—though he had to admit he didn't mind the publicity—than for love. His ancestors had fought under one name or another—viking, Crusader, mercenary, rebel, patriot, whatever was fashionable at the moment. Struggle was in his blood, and in these degenerate days there was little struggle against save what he hunted.

Well—tomorrow—he drifted off to sleep.

He woke in the short gray dawn, made a quick breakfast, and whistled his hound to heel. His nostrils dilated with excitement, a high keen drunkenness that sang wonderfully within him. Today—maybe today!

They had to take a roundabout way down into the canyon and the hound cast about for an hour before he picked up the scent. Then the deep-voiced cry rose again and they were off—more slowly now, for it was a cruel stony trail.

The sun climbed high as they worked along the ancient river-bed. Its pale chill light washed needle-sharp crags and fantastically painted cliffs, shale and sand and the wreck of geological ages. The low harsh brush crunched under the man's feet, writhing and crackling its impotent protest. Otherwise it was still, a deep and taut and somehow waiting stillness.

The hound shattered the quiet with an eager yelp and plunged forward. Hot scent! Riordan dashed after him, trampling through dense bush, panting and swearing and grinning with excitement.

Suddenly the brush opened underfoot. With a howl of dismay, the hound slid down the sloping wall of the pit it had covered. Riordan flung himself forward with tigerish swiftness, flat down on his belly with one hand barely catching the animal's tail. The shock almost pulled him into the hole too. He wrapped one arm around a bush that clawed at his helmet and pulled the hound back.

Shaking, he peered into the trap. It had been well made—about twenty feet deep, with walls as straight and narrow as the sand would allow, and skillfully covered with brush. Planted in the bottom were three wicked-looking flint spears. Had he been a shade less quick in his reactions, he would have lost the hound and perhaps himself.

He skinned his teeth in a wolf-grin and looked around. The owlie must have worked all night on it. Then he couldn't be far away—and he'd be very tired—

As if to answer his thoughts, a boulder crashed down from the nearer cliff wall. It was a monster, but a falling object on Mars has less than half the acceleration it does on Earth. Riordan scrambled aside as it boomed onto the place where he had been lying.

"Come on!" he yelled, and plunged toward the cliff.

For an instant a gray form loomed over the edge, hurled a spear at him. Riordan snapped a shot at it, and it vanished. The spear glanced off the tough fabric of his suit and he scrambled up a narrow ledge to the top of the precipice.

The Martian was nowhere in sight, but a faint red trail led into the rugged hill country. *Winged him, by God!* The hound was slower in negotiating the shale-covered trail; his own feet were bleeding when he came up. Riordan cursed him and they set out again.

They followed the trail for a mile or two and then it ended. Riordan looked around the wilderness of trees and needles which blocked view in any direction. Obviously the owlie had backtracked and climbed up one of those rocks, from which he could take a flying leap to some other point. But which one?

Sweat which he couldn't wipe off ran down the man's face and body. He twitched intolerably, and his lungs were raw from gasping as his dole of air. But still he laughed in gusty delight. What a chase! What a chase!

Kreega lay in the shadow of a tall rock and shuddered with weariness. Beyond the shade, the sunlight danced in what to him was a blinding, intolerable dazzle, hot and cruel and life-hungry, hard and bright as the metal of the conquerors.

It had been a mistake to spend priceless hours when he might have been resting working on that trap. It hadn't worked, and he might have known that it wouldn't. And now he was hungry, and thirst was like a wild beast in his mouth and throat, and still they followed him.

They weren't far behind now. All this day they had been dogging him; he had never been more than half an hour ahead. No rest, no rest, a devil's hunt through a tormented wilderness of stone and sand, and now he could only wait for the battle with an iron burden of exhaustion laid on him.

The wound in his side burned. It wasn't deep, but it had cost him blood and pain and the few minutes of catnapping he might have snatched.

For a moment, the warrior Kreega was gone and a lonely, frightened infant sobbed in the desert silence. *Why can't they let me alone?*

A low, dusty-green bush rustled. A sandrunner piped in one of the ravines. They were getting close.

Wearily, Kreega scrambled up on top of the rock and crouched low. He had backtracked to it; they should by rights go past him toward his tower.

He could see it from here, a low yellow ruin worn by the winds of millennia. There had only been time to dart in, snatch a bow and a few arrows and an axe. Pitiful weapons—the arrows could not penetrate the Earthman's suit when there was only a Martian's thin grasp to draw the bow, and even with a steel head the axe was a small and feeble thing. But it was all he had, he and his few little allies of a desert which fought only to keep its solitude.

Repatriated slaves had told him of the Earthlings' power. Their roaring machines filled the silence of their own deserts, gouged the quiet face of their own moon, shook the planets with a senseless fury of meaningless energy. They were the conquerors, and it never occurred to them that an ancient peace and stillness could be worth preserving.

Well—he fitted an arrow to the string and crouched in the silent, flimmering sunlight, waiting.

The hound came first, yelping and howling. Kreega drew the bow as far as he could. But the human had to come near first—

There he came, running and bounding over the rocks, rifle in hand and restless eyes shining with taut green light, closing in for the death. Kreega swung softly around. The beast was beyond the rock now, the Earthman almost below it.

The bow twanged. With a savage thrill, Kreega saw the arrow go through the hound, saw the creature leap in the air and then roll over and over, howling and biting at the thing in its breast.

Like a gray thunderbolt, the Martian launched himself off the rock, down at the human. If his axe could shatter that helmet—

He struck the man and they went down together. Wildly, the Martian hewed. The axe glanced off the plastic—he hadn't had room for a swing. Riordan roared and lashed out with a fist. Retching, Kreega rolled backward.

Riordan snapped a shot at him. Kreega turned and fled. The man got to one knee, sighting carefully on the gray form that streaked up the nearest slope.

A little sandsnake darted up the man's leg and wrapped about his wrist. Its small strength was just enough to pull the gun aside. The bullet screamed past Kreega's ear as he vanished into a cleft.

He felt the thin death-agony of the snake as the man pulled it loose and crushed it underfoot. Somewhat later, he heard a dull boom echoing between the hills. The man had gotten explosives from his boat and blown up the tower.

He had lost axe and bow. Now he was utterly weaponless, without even a place to retire for a last stand. And the hunter would not give up. Even without his animals, he would follow, more slowly but as relentlessly as before.

Kreega collapsed on a shelf of rock. Dry sobbing racked his thin body, and the sunset wind cried with him.

Presently he looked up, across a red and yellow immensity to the low sun. Long shadows were creeping over the land, peace and stillness for a brief moment before the iron cold of night closed down. Somewhere the soft trill of a sandrunner echoed between low wind-worn cliffs, and the brush began to speak, whispering back and forth in its ancient wordless tongue.

The desert, the planet and its wind and sand under the high cold stars, the clean open land of silence and loneliness and a destiny which was not man's, spoke to him. The enormous oneness of life on Mars, drawn together against the cruel environment, stirred in his blood. As the sun went down and the stars blossomed forth in awesome frosty glory, Kreega began to think again.

He did not hate his persecutor, but the grimness of Mars was in him. He fought the war of all which was old and primitive and lost in its own dreams against the alien and the desecrator. It was as ancient and pitiless as life, that war, and each battle won or lost meant something even if no one ever heard of it.

You do not fight alone, whispered the desert. *You fight for all Mars, and we are with you.*

Something moved in the darkness, a tiny warm

form running across his hand, a little feathered mouse-like thing that burrowed under the sand and lived its small fugitive life and was glad in its own way of living. But it was a part of a world, and Mars has no pity in its voice.

Still, a tenderness was within Kreega's heart, and he whispered gently in the language that was not a language, *You will do this for us? You will do it, little brother?*

Riordan was too tired to sleep well. He had lain awake for a long time, thinking, and that is not good for a man alone in the Martian hills.

So now the rockhound was dead too. It didn't matter, the owlie wouldn't escape. But somehow the incident brought home to him the immensity and the age and the loneliness of the desert.

It whispered to him. The brush rustled and something wailed in darkness and the wind blew with a wild mournful sound over faintly starlit cliffs, and it was as if they all somehow had voice, as if the whole world muttered and threatened him in the night. Dimly, he wondered if man would ever subdue Mars, if the human race had not finally run across something bigger than itself.

But that was nonsense. Mars was old and worn-out and barren, dreaming itself into slow death. The tramp of human feet, shouts of men, and roar of sky-storming rockets, were waking it, but to a new destiny, to man's. When Ares lifted its hard spires above the hills of Syrtis, where then were the ancient gods of Mars?

It was cold, and the cold deepened as the night wore on. The stars were fire and ice, glittering diamonds in the deep crystal dark. Now and then he could hear a faint snapping borne through the earth as rock or tree split open. The wind laid itself to rest, sound froze to death, there was only the hard clear starlight falling through space to shatter on the ground.

Once something stirred. He woke from a restless sleep and saw a small thing skittering toward him. He groped for the rifle beside his sleeping bag, then laughed harshly. It was only a sandmouse. But it proved that the Martian had no chance of sneaking up on him while he rested.

He didn't laugh again. The sound had echoed too hollowly in his helmet.

With the clear bitter dawn he was up. He wanted to get the hunt over with. He was dirty and unshaven inside the unit, sick of iron rations pushed through the airlock, stiff and sore with exertion. Lacking the hound, which he'd had to shoot, tracking would be slow, but he didn't want to go back to Port Armstrong for another. No, hell take that Martian, he'd have the devil's skin soon!

Breakfast and a little moving made him feel better. He looked with a practiced eye for the Martian's trail. There was sand and brush over everything, even the rocks had a thin coating of their own erosion. The owlie couldn't cover his tracks perfectly—if he tried, it would slow him too much. Riordan fell into a steady jog.

Noon found him on higher ground, rough hills with gaunt needles of rock reaching yards into the sky. He kept going, confident of his own ability to wear down the quarry. He'd run deer to earth back home, day after day until the animal's heart broke and it waited quivering for him to come.

The trail looked clear and fresh now. He tensed with the knowledge that the Martian couldn't be far away.

Too clear! Could this be bait for another trap? He hefted the rifle and proceeded more warily. But no, there wouldn't have been time—

He mounted a high ridge and looked over the grim, fantastic landscape. Near the horizon he saw a blackened strip, the border of his radioactive barrier. The Martian couldn't go further, and if he doubled back Riordan would have an excellent chance of spotting him.

He turned up his speaker and let his voice roar into the stillness: "Come out, owlie! I'm going to get you, you might as well come out now and be done with it!"

The echoes took it up, flying back and forth between the naked crags, trembling and shivering under the brassy arch of sky. *Come out, come out, come out—*

The Martian seemed to appear from thin air, a gray ghost rising out of the jumbled stones and standing poised not twenty feet away. For an instant, the shock of it was too much. Riordan gaped in disbelief. Kreega waited, quivering ever so faintly as if he were a mirage.

Then the man shouted and lifted his rifle. Still the Martian stood there as if carved in gray stone, and with a shock of disappointment Riordan thought that he had, after all, decided to give himself to an inevitable death.

Well, it had been a good hunt. "So long," whispered Riordan, and squeezed the trigger.

Since the sandmouse had crawled into the barrel, the gun exploded.

Riordan heard the roar and saw the barrel peel open like a rotten banana. He wasn't hurt, but as he staggered back from the shock Kreega lunged at him.

The Martian was four feet tall, and skinny and weaponless, but he hit the Earthling like a small tornado. His legs wrapped around the man's waist and his hands got to work on the airhose.

Riordan went down under the impact. He snarled, tigerishly, and fastened his hands on the Martian's narrow throat. Kreega snapped futilely at him with his beak. They rolled over in a cloud of dust. The brush began to chatter excitedly.

Riordan tried to break Kreega's neck—the Martian twisted away, bored in again.

With a shock of terror, the man heard the hiss of escaping air as Kreega's beak and fingers finally worried the airhose loose. An automatic valve clamped shut, but there was no connection with the pump now—

Riordan cursed, and got his hands about the Martian's throat again. Then he simply lay there, squeezing, and not all Kreega's writhing and twistings could break that grip.

Riordan smiled sleepily and held his hands in place. After five minutes or so Kreega was still. Riordan kept right on throttling him for another five minutes, just to make sure. Then he let go and fumbled at his back, trying to reach the pump.

The air in his suit was hot and foul. He couldn't

quite reach around to connect the hose to the pump—

Poor design, he thought vaguely. *But then, these airsuits weren't meant for battle armor*.

He looked at the slight, silent form of the Martian. A faint breeze ruffled the gray feathers. What a fighter the little guy had been! He'd be the pride of the trophy room, back on Earth.

Let's see now—He unrolled his sleeping bag and spread it carefully out. He'd never make it to the rocket with what air he had, so it was necessary to let the suspensine into his suit. But he'd have to get inside the bag, lest the nights freeze his blood solid.

He crawled in, fastening the flaps carefully, and opened the valve on the suspensine tank. Lucky he had it—but then, a good hunter thinks of everything. He'd get awfully bored, lying here till Wisby caught the signal in ten days or so and came to find him, but he'd last. It would be an experience to remember. In this dry air, the Martian's skin would keep perfectly well.

He felt the paralysis creep up on him, the waning of heartbeat and lung action. His senses and mind were still alive, and he grew aware that complete relaxation has its unpleasant aspects. Oh, well—he'd won. He'd killed the wiliest game with his own hands.

Presently Kreega sat up. He felt himself gingerly. There seemed to be a rib broken—well, that could be fixed. He was still alive. He'd been choked for a good ten minutes, but a Martian can last fifteen without air.

He opened the sleeping bag and got Riordan's

keys. Then he limped slowly back to the rocket. A day or two of experimentation taught him how to fly it. He'd go to his kinsmen near Syrtis. Now that they had an Earthly machine, and Earthly weapons to copy—

But there was other business first. He didn't hate Riordan, but Mars is a hard world. He went back and dragged the Earthling into a cave and hid him beyond all possibility of human search parties finding him.

For a while he looked into the man's eyes. Horror stared dumbly back at him. He spoke slowly, in halting English: "For those you killed, and for being a stranger on a world that does not want you, and against the day when Mars is free, I leave you."

Before departing, he got several oxygen tanks from the boat and hooked them into the man's air supply. That was quite a bit of air for one in suspended animation. Enough to keep him alive for a thousand years.

THE STAR BEAST

he rebirth technician thought he had heard everything in the course of some three centuries. ut he was astonished now.

"My dear fellow—" he said. "Did you say a ger?"

"That's right," said Harol. "You can do it, can't ou?"

"Well—I suppose so. I'd have to study the problem first, of course. Nobody has ever wanted a ebirth that far from human. But offhand I'd say it as possible." The technician's eyes lit with a leam which had not been there for many dec-les. "It would at least be—interesting!"

"I think you already have a record of a tiger," id Harol.

"Oh, we must have. We have records of every limal still extant when the technique was invented, and I'm sure there must still have been a few tigers around then. But it's a problem of modification. A human mind just can't exist in a nervous system that different. We'd have to change the record enough—larger brain with more convolutions, of course, and so on. . . . Even then it'd be far from perfect, but your basic mentality should be stable for a year or two, barring accidents. That's all the time you'd want anyway, isn't it?"

"I suppose so," said Harol.

"Rebirth in animal forms is getting fashionable these days," admitted the technician. "But so far they've only wanted animals with easily modified systems. Anthropoid apes, now—you don't even have to change a chimpanzee's brain at all for it to hold a stable human mentality for years. Elephants are good too. But—a tiger—" He shook his head. "I suppose it can be done, after a fashion. But why not a gorilla."

"I want a carnivore," said Harol.

"Your psychiatrist, I suppose—" hinted the technician.

Harol nodded curtly. The technician sighed and gave up the hope of juicy confessions. A worker at Rebirth Station heard a lot of strange stories, but this fellow wasn't giving. Oh, well, the mere fact of his demand would furnish gossip for days.

"When can it be ready?" asked Harol.

The technician scratched his head thoughtfully. "It'll take a while," he said. "We have to get the record scanned, you know, and work out a basic neural pattern that'll hold the human mind. It's more than a simple memory-superimposition. The genes control an organism all through its lifespan, dictating, within the limits of environment, even the time and speed of aging. You can't have an animal with an ontogeny entirely opposed to its basic phylogeny—it wouldn't be viable. So we'll have to modify the very molecules of the cells, as well as the gross anatomy of the nervous system."

"In short," smiled Harol, "this intelligent tiger will breed true."

"If it found a similar tigress," answered the technician. "Not a real one—there aren't any left, and besides, the heredity would be too different. But maybe you want a female body for someone?"

"No, I only want a body for myself." Briefly, Harol thought of Avi and tried to imagine her incarnated in the supple, deadly grace of the huge cat. But no, she wasn't the type. And solitude was part of the therapy anyway.

"Once we have the modified record, of course, there's nothing to superimposing your memory patterns on it," said the technician. "That'll be just the usual process, like any human rebirth. But to make up that record—well, I can put the special scanning and computing units over at Research on the problem. Nobody's working there. Say a week. Will that do?"

"Fine," said Harol. "I'll be back in a week."

He turned with a brief good-by and went down the long slideway toward the nearest transmitter. It was almost deserted now save for the unhuman forms of mobile robots gliding on their errands. The faint, deep hum of activity which filled Rebirth Station was almost entirely that of machines, of electronic flows whispering through vacuum, the silent cerebration of artificial intellects so far surpassing those of their human creators that men could no longer follow their thoughts. A human brain simply couldn't operate with that many simultaneous factors.

The machines were the latter-day oracles. And the life-giving gods. *We're parasites on our machines,* thought Harol. *We're little fleas hopping around on the giants we created, once. There are no real human scientists any more. How can there be, when the electronic brains and the great machines which are their bodies can do it all so much quicker and better—can do things we would never even have dreamed of, things of which man's highest geniuses have only the faintest glimmer of an understanding? That has paralyzed us, that and the rebirth immortality. Now there's nothing left but a life of idleness and a round of pleasure—and how much fun is anything after centuries?*

It was no wonder that animal rebirth was all the rage. It offered some prospect of novelty—for a while.

He passed a mirror and paused to look at himself. There was nothing unusual about him; he had the tall body and handsome features that were uniform today. There was a little gray at his temples and he was getting a bit bald on top, though this body was only thirty-five. But then it always had aged early. In the old days, he'd hardly have reached a hundred.

I am—let me see—four hundred and sixty-three years old. At least, my memory is—and what am I, the essential I, but a memory track?

Unlike most of the people in the building, he

wore clothes, a light tunic and cloak. He was a little sensitive about the flabbiness of his body. He really should keep himself in better shape. But what was the point of it, really, when his twenty-year-old record was so superb a specimen?

He reached the transmitter booth and hesitated a moment, wondering where to go. He could go home—have to get his affairs in order before undertaking the tiger phase—or he could drop in on Avi or—His mind wandered away until he came to himself with an angry start. After four and a half centuries, it was getting hard to coördinate all his memories; he was becoming increasingly absent-minded. Have to get the psychostaff at Rebirth to go over his record, one of these generations, and eliminate some of that useless clutter from his synapses.

He decided to visit Avi. As he spoke her name to the transmitter and waited for it to hunt through the electronics files at Central for her current residence, the thought came that in all his lifetime he had only twice seen Rebirth Station from the outside. The place was immense, a featureless pile rearing skyward above the almost empty European forests—as impressive a sight, in its way, as Tycho Crater or the rings of Saturn. But when the transmitter sent you directly from booth to booth, inside the buildings, you rarely had occasion to look at their exteriors.

For a moment he toyed with the thought of having himself transmitted to some nearby house just to see the Station. But—oh, well, any time in the next few millennia. The Station would last forever, and so would he.

The transmitter field was generated. At the speed of light, Harol flashed around the world to Avi's dwelling.

The occasion was ceremonial enough for Ramacan to put on his best clothes, a red cloak over his tunic and the many jeweled ornaments prescribed for formal wear. Then he sat down by his transmitter and waited.

The booth stood just inside the colonnaded verandah. From his seat, Ramacan could look through the open doors to the great slopes and peaks of the Caucasus, green now with returning summer save where the everlasting snows flashed under a bright sky. He had lived here for many centuries, contrary to the restlessness of most Earthlings. But he liked the place. It had a quiet immensity; it never changed. Most humans these days sought variety, a feverish quest for the new and untasted, old minds in young bodies trying to recapture a lost freshness. Ramacan was—they called him stodgy, probably. Stable or steady might be closer to the truth. Which made him ideal for his work. Most of what government remained on Earth was left to him.

Felgi was late. Ramacan didn't worry about it, he was never in a hurry himself. But when the Procyonite did arrive, the manner of it brought an amazed oath even from the Earthling.

He didn't come through the transmitter. He came in a boat from his ship, a lean metal shark drifting out of the sky and sighing to the lawn. Ramacan noticed the flat turrets and the ominous muzzles of guns projecting from them. Anachronism—Sol hadn't seen a warship for more centuries than he could remember. But—

Felgi came out of the airlock. He was followed by a squad of armed guards, who grounded their blasters and stood to stiff attention. The Procyonite captain walked alone up to the house.

Ramacan had met him before, but he studied the man with a new attention. Like most in his fleet, Felgi was a little undersized by Earthly standards, and the rigidity of his face and posture were almost shocking. His severe, form-fitting black uniform differed little from those of his subordinates except for insignia of his rank. His features were gaunt, dark with the protective pigmentation necessary under the terrible blaze of Procyon, and there was something in his eyes which Ramacan had never seen before.

The Procyonites looked human enough. But Ramacan wondered if there was any truth to those rumors which had been flying about Earth since their arrival, that mutation and selection during their long and cruel stay had changed the colonists into something that could never have been at home.

Certainly their social setup and their basic psychology seemed to be—foreign.

Felgi came up the short escalator to the verandah and bowed stiffly. The psychographs had taught him modern Terrestrial, but his voice still held an echo of the harsh colonial tongue and his phrasing was strange: "Greeting to you, Commander."

Ramacan returned the bow, but his was the elaborate sweeping gesture of Earth. "Be welcome, Gen—ah—General Felgi." Then, informally: "Please come in."

"Thank you." The other man walked into the house.

"Your companions—?"

"My *men* will remain outside." Felgi sat down without being invited, a serious breach of etiquette—but after all, the mores of his home were different.

"As you wish." Ramacan dialed for drinks on the room creator.

"No," said Felgi.

"Pardon me?"

"We don't drink at Procyon. I thought you knew that."

"Pardon me. I had forgotten." Regretfully, Ramacan let the wine and glasses return to the matter bank and sat down.

Felgi sat with steely erectness, making the efforts of the seat to mold itself to his contours futile. Slowly, Ramacan recognized the emotion that crackled and smoldered behind the dark lean visage.

Anger.

"I trust you are finding your stay on Earth pleasant," he said into the silence.

"Let us not make meaningless words," snapped Felgi. "I am here on business."

"As you wish." Ramacan tried to relax, but he couldn't; his nerves and muscles were suddenly tight.

"As far as I can gather," said Felgi, "you head the government of Sol."

"I suppose you could say that. I have the title of Coördinator. But there isn't much to coördinate these days. Our social system practically runs itself."

"Insofar as you have one. But actually you are completely disorganized. Every individual seems to be sufficient to himself."

"Naturally. When everyone owns a matter creator which can supply all his ordinary needs, there is bound to be economic and thus a large degree of social independence. We have public services, of course—Rebirth Station, Power Station, Transmitter Central, and a few others. But there aren't many."

"I cannot see why you aren't overwhelmed by crime." The last word was necessarily Procyonian, and Ramacan raised his eyebrows puzzledly. "Antisocial behavior," explained Felgi irritably. "Theft, murder, destruction."

"What possible need has anyone to steal?" asked Ramacan, surprised. "And the present degree of independence virtually eliminates social friction. Actual psychoses have been removed from the neural components of the rebirth records long ago."

"At any rate, I assume you speak for Sol."

"How can I speak for almost a billion different people? I have little authority, you know. So little is needed. However, I'll do all I can if you'll only tell me—"

"The decadence of Sol is incredible," snapped Felgi.

"You may be right." Ramacan's tone was mild, but he bristled under the urbane surface. "I've sometimes thought so myself. However, what has that to do with the present subject of discussion—whatever it may be?"

"You left us in exile," said Felgi, and now the wrath and hate were edging his voice, glittering out of his eyes. "For nine hundred years, Earth lived in luxury while the humans on Procyon fought and suffered and died in the worst kind of hell."

"What reason was there for us to go to Procyon?" asked Ramacan. "After the first few ships had established a colony there—well, we had a whole galaxy before us. When no colonial ships came from your star, I suppose it was assumed the people there had died off. Somebody should perhaps have gone there to check up, but it took twenty years to get there and it was an inhospitable and unrewarding system and there was so many other stars. Then the matter creator came along and Sol no longer had a government to look after such things. Space travel became an individual business, and no individual was interested in Procyon." He shrugged. "I'm sorry."

"You're *sorry!*" Felgi spat the words out. "For nine hundred years our ancestors fought the bitterness of their planets, starved and died in misery, sank back almost to barbarism and had to slug their way every step back upwards, waged the cruelest war of history with the Czernigi—unending centuries of war until one race or the other should be exterminated. We died of old age, generation after generation of us—we wrung our needs out of planets never meant for humans—my ship spent twenty years getting back here, twenty years of short human lives—and you're sorry!"

He sprang up and paced the floor, his bitter voice lashing out. "You've had the stars, you've had immortality, you've had everything which can be made of matter. And *we* spent twenty years cramped up in metal walls to get here—wondering if perhaps Sol hadn't fallen on evil times and needed our help!"

"What would you have us do now?" demanded Ramacan. "All Earth has made you welcome—"

"We're a novelty!"

"—all Earth is ready to offer you all it can. What more do you want of us?"

For a moment the rage was still in Felgi's strange eyes. Then it faded, blinked out as if he had drawn a curtain across them, and he stood still and spoke with sudden quietness. "True. I—I should apologize, I suppose. The nervous strain—"

"Don't mention it," said Ramacan. But inwardly he wondered. Just how far could he trust the Procyonites? All those hard centuries of war and intrigue—and then they weren't really human any more, not the way Earth's dwellers were human—but what else could he do? "It's quite all right. I understand."

"Thank you." Felgi sat down again. "May I ask what you offer?"

"Duplicate matter creators, of course. And robots duplicated to administer the more complex Rebirth techniques. Certain of the processes involved are beyond the understanding of the human mind."

"I'm not sure it would be a good thing for us," said Felgi. "Sol has gotten stagnant. There doesn't seem to have been any significant change in the last half millennium. Why, our spaceship drives are better than yours."

"What do you expect?" shrugged Ramacan. "What

possible incentive have we for change? Progress, to use an archaic term, is a means to an end, and we have reached its goal."

"I still don't know—" Felgi rubbed his chin. "I'm not even sure how your duplicators work."

"I can't tell you much about them. But the greatest technical mind on Earth can't tell you everything. As I told you before, the whole thing is just too immense for real knowledge. Only the electronic brains can handle so much at once."

"Maybe you could give me a short résumé of it, and tell me just what your setup is. I'm especially interested in the actual means by which it's put to use."

"Well, let me see." Ramacan searched his memory. "The ultrawave was discovered—oh, it must be a good seven or eight hundred years ago now. It carries energy, but it's not electromagnetic. The theory of it, as far as any human can follow it, ties in with wave mechanics.

"The first great application came with the discovery that ultrawaves transmit over distances of many astronomical units, unhindered by intervening matter, and with *no energy loss*. The theory of that has been interpreted as meaning that the wave is, well, I suppose you could say it's 'aware' of the receiver and only goes to it. There must be a receiver as well as a transmitter to generate the wave. Naturally, that led to a perfectly efficient power transmitter. Today all the Solar System gets its energy from the Sun—transmitted by the Power Station on the day side of Mercury. Everything from interplanetary spaceships to televisors and clocks runs from that power source."

"Sounds dangerous to me," said Felgi. "Suppose the station fails?"

"It won't," said Ramacan confidently. "The Station has its own robots, no human technicians at all. Everything is recorded. If any one part goes wrong, it is automatically dissolved into the nearest matter bank and recreated. There are other safeguards too. The Station has never given trouble since it was first built."

"I see—" Felgi's tone was thoughtful.

"Soon thereafter," said Ramacan, "it was found that the ultrawave could also transmit matter. Circuits could be built which would scan any body atom by atom, dissolve it to energy, and transmit this energy on the ultrawave along with the scanning signal. At the receiver, of course, the process is reversed. I'm grossly oversimplifying, naturally. It's not a mere signal which is involved, but a fantastic complex of signals such as only the ultrawave could carry. However, you get the general idea. Just about all transportation today is by this technique. Vehicles for air or space exist only for very special purposes and for pleasure trips."

"You have some kind of controlling center for this too, don't you?"

"Yes. Transmitter Station, on Earth, is in Brazil. It holds all the records of such things as addresses, and it coördinates the millions of units all over the planet. It's a huge, complicated affair, of course, but perfectly efficient. Since distance no longer means anything, it's most practical to centralize the public-service units.

"Well, from transmission it was but a step to

recording the signal and reproducing it out of a bank of any other matter. So—the duplicator. The matter creator. You can imagine what that did to Sol's economy! Today everybody owns one, and if he doesn't have a record of what he wants he can have one duplicated and transmitted from Creator Station's great 'library.' Anything whatsoever in the way of material goods is his for the turning of a dial and the flicking of a switch.

"And this, in turn, soon led to the Rebirth technique. It's but an extension of all that has gone before. Your body is recorded at its prime of life, say around twenty years of age. Then you live for as much longer as you care to, say to thirty-five or forty or whenever you begin to get a little old. Then your neural pattern is recorded alone by special scanning units. Memory, as you surely know, is a matter of neural synapses and altered protein molecules, not too difficult to scan and record. This added pattern is superimposed electronically on the record of your twenty-year-old body. Then your own body is used as the matter bank for materializing the pattern in the altered record and—virtually instantaneously—your young body is created—but with all the memories of the old! You're—Immortal!"

"In a way," said Felgi. "But it still doesn't seem right to me. The ego, the soul, whatever you want to call it—it seems as if you lose that. You create simply a perfect copy."

"When the copy is so perfect it cannot be told from the original," said Ramacan, "then what *is* the difference? The ego is essentially a matter of continuity. You, your essential self, are a constantly changing pattern of synapses bearing only a temporary relationship to the molecules that happen to carry the pattern at the moment. It is the design, not the structural material, that is important. And it is the design that we preserve."

"Do you?" asked Felgi. "I seemed to notice a strong likeness among Earthlings."

"Well, since the records can be altered there was no reason for us to carry around crippled or diseased or deformed bodies," said Ramacan. "Records could be made of perfect specimens and *all* ego-patterns wiped from them; then someone else's neural pattern could be superimposed. Rebirth—in a new body! Naturally, everyone would want to match the prevailing beauty standard, and so a certain uniformity has appeared. A different body would of course lead in time to a different personality, man being a psychosomatic unit. But the continuity which is the essential attribute of the ego would still be there."

"Ummm—I see. May I ask how old you are?"

"About seven hundred and fifty. I was middle-aged when Rebirth was established, but I had myself put into a young body."

Felgi's eyes went from Ramacan's smooth, youthful face to his own hands, with the knobby joints and prominent veins of his sixty years. Briefly, the fingers tightened, but his voice remained soft. "Don't you have trouble keeping your memories straight?"

"Yes, but every so often I have some of the useless and repetitious ones taken out of the record, and that helps. The robots know exactly what part of the pattern corresponds to a given memory and can erase it. After, say, another thousand years, I'll probably have big gaps. But they won't be important."

"How about the apparent acceleration of time with age?"

"That was bad after the first couple of centuries, but then it seemed to flatten out, the nervous system adapted to it. I must say, though," admitted Ramacan, "that it as well as lack of incentive is probably responsible for our present static society and general unproductiveness. There's a terrible tendency to procrastination, and a day seems too short a time to get anything done."

"The end of progress, then—of science, of art, of striving, of all which has made man human."

"Not so. We still have our arts and handicrafts and—hobbies, I suppose you could call them. Maybe we don't do so much any more, but—why should we?"

"I'm surprised at finding so much of Earth gone back to wilderness. I should think you'd be badly overcrowded."

"Not so. The creator and the transmitter make it possible for men to live far apart, in physical distance, and still be in as close touch as necessary. Communities are obsolete. As for the population problem, there isn't any. After a few children, not many people want more. It's sort of, well, unfashionable anyway."

"That's right," said Felgi quietly, "I've hardly seen a child on Earth."

"And of course there's a slow drift out to the stars as people seek novelty. You can send your recording in a robot ship, and a journey of centuries becomes nothing. I suppose that's another reason for the tranquility of Earth. The more restless and adventurous elements have moved away."

"Have you any communication with them?"

"None. Not when spaceships can only go at half the speed of light. Once in a while curious wanderers will drop in on us, but it's very rare. They seem to be developing some strange cultures out in the galaxy."

"Don't you do *any* work on Earth?"

"Oh, some public services must be maintained— psychiatry, human technicians to oversee various stations, and so on. And then there are any number of personal-service enterprises—entertainment, especially, and the creation of intricate handicrafts for the creators to duplicate. But there are enough people willing to work a few hours a month or week, if only to fill in their time or to get the credit-balance which will enable them to purchase such services for themselves if they desire.

"It's a perfectly stable culture, General Felgi. It's perhaps the only really stable society in all human history."

"I wonder—haven't you any precautions at all?" Any military forces, any defenses against invaders— *anything?*"

"Why in the cosmos should we fear that?" exclaimed Ramacan. "Who would come invading over light-years—at half the speed of light? Or if they did, *why?*"

"Plunder—"

Ramacan laughed. "We could duplicate anything they asked for and give it to them."

"Could you, now?" Suddenly Felgi stood up. "Could you?"

Ramacan rose too, with his nerves and muscles tightening again. There was a hard triumph in the Procyonite's face, vindictive, threatening.

Felgi signaled to his men through the door. They trotted up on the double, and their blasters were raised and something hard and ugly was in their eyes.

"Coördinator Ramacan," said Felgi, "you are under arrest."

"What—what—" The Earthling felt as if someone had struck him a physical blow. He clutched for support. Vaguely he heard the iron tones:

"You've confirmed what I thought. Earth is unarmed, unprepared, helplessly dependent on a few undefended key spots. And I captain a warship of space filled with soldiers.

"We're taking over!"

Avi's current house lay in North America, on the middle Atlantic seaboard. Like most private homes these days, it was small and low-ceilinged, with adjustable interior walls and furnishings for easy variegation. She loved flowers, and great brilliant gardens bloomed around her dwelling, down toward the sea and landward to the edge of the immense forest which had returned with the end of agriculture.

They walked between the shrubs and trees and blossoms, she and Harol. Her unbound hair was long and bright in the sea breeze, her eighteen-year-old form was slim and graceful as a young deer's. Suddenly he hated the thought of leaving her.

"I'll miss you, Harol," she said.

He smiled lopsidedly. "You'll get over that," he said. "There are others. I suppose you'll be looking up some of those spacemen they say arrived from Procyon a few days ago."

"Of course," she said innocently. "I'm surprised you don't stay around and try for some of the women they had along. It would be a change."

"Not much of a change," he answered. "Frankly, I'm at a loss to understand the modern passion for variety. One person seems very much the same as another in that regard."

"It's a matter of companionship," she said. "After not too many years of living with someone, you get to know him too well. You can tell exactly what he's going to do, what he'll say to you, what he'll have for dinner, and what sort of show he'll want to go to in the evening. These colonists will be—new! They'll have other ways from ours, they'll be able to tell of a new, different planetary system, they'll—" She broke off. "But now so many women will be after the strangers, I doubt if I'll have a chance."

"But if it's conversation you want—oh, well." Harol shrugged. "Anyway, I understand the Procyonites still have family relationships. They'll be quite jealous of their women. And I need this change."

"A carnivore—!" Avi laughed, and Harol thought again what music it was. "You have an original mind, at least." Suddenly she was earnest. She

held both his hands and looked close into his eyes.
"That's always been what I liked about you, Harol.
You've always been a thinker and adventurer, you've
never let yourself grow mentally lazy like most of
us. After we've been apart for a few years, you're
always new again, you've gotten out of your rut
and done something strange, you've learned something different, you've grown young again. We've
always come back to each other, dear, and I've
always been glad of it."

"And I," he said quietly. "Though I've regretted
the separations too." He smiled, a wry smile with
a tinge of sorrow behind it. "We could have been
very happy in the old days, Avi. We would have
been married and together for life."

"A few years, and then age and feebleness and
death." She shuddered. "Death! Nothingness! Not
even the world can exist when one is dead. Not
when you've no brain left to know about it. Just—
nothing. As if you had never been! Haven't you
ever been afraid of the thought?"

"No," he said, and kissed her.

"That's another way you're different," she murmured. "I wonder why you never went out to the
stars, Harol. All your children did."

"I asked you to go with me, once."

"Not I. I like it here. Life is fun, Harol. I don't
seem to get bored as easily as most people. But
that isn't answering my question."

"Yes, it is," he said, and then clamped his mouth
shut.

He stood looking at her, wondering if he was
the last man on Earth who loved a woman, won-

dering how she really felt about him. Perhaps, in her way, she loved him—they always came back to each other. But not in the way he cared for her, not so that being apart was a gnawing pain and reunion was— No matter.

"I'll still be around," he said. "I'll be wandering through the woods here; I'll have the Rebirth men transmit me back to your house and then I'll be in the neighborhood."

"My pet tiger," she smiled. "Come around to see me once in a while, Harol. Come with me to some of the parties."

A nice spectacular ornament— "No, thanks. But you can scratch my head and feed me big bloody steaks, and I'll arch my back and purr."

They walked hand in hand toward the beach. "What made you decide to be a tiger?" she asked.

"My psychiatrist recommended an animal rebirth," he replied. "I'm getting terribly neurotic, Avi. I can't sit still five minutes and I get gloomy spells where nothing seems worthwhile any more, life is a dready farce and—well, it seems to be becoming a rather common disorder these days. Essentially it's boredom. When you have everything without working for it, life can become horribly flat. When you've lived for centuries, tried it all hundreds of times—no change, no real excitement, nothing to call forth all that's in you— Anyway, the doctor suggested I go to the stars. When I refused that, he suggested I change to animal for a while. But I didn't want to be like everyone else. Not an ape or an elephant."

"Same old contrary Harol," she murmured, and kissed him. He responded with unexpected violence.

"A year or two of wild life, in a new and unhuman body, will make all the difference," he said after a while. They lay on the sand, feeling the sunlight wash over them, hearing the lullaby of waves and smelling the clean, harsh tang of sea and salt and many windy kilometers. High overhead a gull circled, white against the blue.

"Won't you change?" she asked.

"Oh, yes. I won't even be able to remember a lot of things I now know. I doubt if even the most intelligent tiger could understand vector analysis. But that won't matter, I'll get it back when they restore my human form. When I feel the personality change has gone as far as is safe, I'll come here and you can send me back to Rebirth. The important thing is the therapy—a change of viewpoint, a new and challenging environment— Avi!" He sat up, on one elbow and looked down at her. "Avi, why don't you come along? Why don't we both become tigers?"

"And have lots of little tigers?" she smiled drowsily. "No, thanks, Harol. Maybe some day, but not now. I'm really not an adventurous person at all." She stretched, and snuggled back against the warm white dune. "I like it the way it is."

And there are those starmen— Sunfire, what's the matter with me? Next thing you know I'll commit an inurbanity against one of her lovers. I need that therapy, all right.

"And then you'll come back and tell me about it," said Avi.

"Maybe not," he teased her. "Maybe I'll find a beautiful tigress somewhere and become so enamored of her I'll never want to change back to human."

"There won't be any tigresses unless you persuade someone else to go along," she answered. "But will you like a human body after having had such a lovely striped skin? Will we poor hairless people still look good to you?"

"Darling," he smiled, "to me you'll always look good enough to eat."

Presently they went back into the house. The sea gull still dipped and soared, high in the sky.

The forest was great and green and mysterious, with sunlight dappling the shadows and a riot of ferns and flowers under the huge old trees. There were brooks tinkling their darkling way between cool, mossy banks, fish leaping like silver streaks in the bright shallows, lonely pools where quiet hung like a mantle, open meadows of wind-rippled grass, space and solitude and an unending pulse of life.

Tiger eyes saw less than human: the world seemed dim and flat and colorless until he got used to it. After that he had increasing difficulty remembering what color and perspective were like. And his other senses came alive, he realized what a captive within his own skull he had been—looking out at a world of which he had never been so real a part as now.

He heard sounds and tones no man had ever perceived, the faint hum and chirr of insects, the rustling of leaves in a light, warm breeze, the vague whisper of an owl's wings, the scurrying of small, frightened creatures through the long grass—

it all blended into a rich symphony, the heartbeat and breath of the forest. And his nostrils quivered to the infinite variety of smells, the heady fragrance of crushed grass, the pungency of fungus and decay, the sharp, wild odor of fur, the hot drunkenness of newly spilled blood. And he felt with every hair, his whiskers quivered to the smallest stirrings, he gloried in the deep, strong play of his muscles—he had come alive, he thought; a man was half dead compared to the vitality that throbbed in the tiger.

At night, at night—there was no darkness for him now. Moonlight was a white, cold blaze through which he stole on feathery feet; the blackest gloom was light to him—shadows, wan patches of luminescence, a shifting, sliding fantasy of gray like an old and suddenly remembered dream.

He laired in a cave he found, and his new body had no discomfort from the damp earth. At night he would stalk out, a huge, dim ghost with only the amber gleam of his eyes for light, and the forest would speak to him with sound and scent and feeling, the taste of game on the wind. He was master then, all the woods shivered and huddled away from him. He was death in black and gold.

Once an ancient poem ran through the human part of his mind, he let the words roll like ominous thunder in his brain and tried to speak them aloud. The forest shivered with the tiger's coughing roar.

Tiger, tiger, burning bright
In the forest of the night,
What immortal hand or eye
Dared frame thy fearful symmetry?

And the arrogant feline soul snarled response: *I did!*

Later he tried to recall the poem, but he couldn't.

At first he was not very successful, too much of his human awkwardness clung to him. He snarled his rage and bafflement when rabbits skittered aside, when a deer scented him lurking and bolted. He went to Avi's house and she fed him big chunks of raw meat and laughed and scratched him under the chin. She was delighted with her pet.

Avi, he thought, and remembered that he loved her. But that was with his human body. To the tiger, she had no esthetic or sexual value. But he liked to let her stroke him, he purred like a mighty engine and rubbed against her slim legs. She was still very dear to him, and when he became human again—

But the tiger's instincts fought their way back; the heritage of a million years was not to be denied no matter how much the technicians had tried to alter him. They had accomplished little more than to increase his intelligence, and the tiger nerves and glands were still there.

The night came when he saw a flock of rabbits dancing in the moonlight and pounced on them. One huge, steely-taloned paw swooped down, he felt the ripping flesh and snapping bone and then he was gulping the sweet, hot blood and peeling the meat from the frail ribs. He went wild, he roared and raged all night, shouting his exultance to the pale frosty moon. At dawn he slunk back to his cave, wearied, his human mind a little ashamed of it all. But the next night he was hunting again.

His first deer! He lay patiently on a branch

overhanging a trail; only his nervous tail moved while the slow hours dragged by, and he waited. And when the doe passed underneath he was on her like a tawny lightning bolt. A great slapping paw, jaws like shears, a brief, terrible struggle, and she lay dead at his feet. He gorged himself, he ate till he could hardly crawl back to the cave, and then he slept like a drunken man until hunger woke him and he went back to the carcass. A pack of wild dogs were devouring it, he rushed on them and killed one and scattered the rest. Thereafter he continued his feast until only bones were left.

The forest was full of game; it was an easy life for a tiger. But not too easy. He never knew whether he would go back with full or empty belly, and that was part of the pleasure.

They had not removed all the tiger memories; fragments remained to puzzle him; sometimes he woke up whimpering with a dim wonder as to where he was and what had happened. He seemed to remember misty jungle dawns, a broad brown river shining under the sun, another cave and another striped form beside him. As time went on he grew confused, he thought vaguely that he must once have hunted sambar and seen the white rhinoceros go by like a moving mountain in the twilight. It was growing harder to keep things straight.

That was, of course, only to be expected. His feline brain could not possibly hold all the memories and concepts of the human, and with the passage of weeks and months he lost the earlier clarity of recollection. He still identified himself with a certain sound, "Harol," and he remembered other forms and scenes—but more and more dimly, as if they were the fading shards of a dream. And he kept firmly in mind that he had to go back to Avi and let her send—take?—him somewhere else before he forgot who he was.

Well, there was time for that, thought the human component. He wouldn't lose that memory all at once, he'd know well in advance that the superimposed human personality was disintegrating in its strange house and that he ought to get back. Meanwhile he grew more and deeply into the forest life, his horizons narrowed until it seemed the whole of existence.

Now and then he wandered down to the sea and Avi's home, to get a meal and be made much of. But the visits grew more and more infrequent, the open country made him nervous and he couldn't stay indoors after dark.

Tiger, tiger—

And summer wore on.

He woke to a raw wet chill in the cave, rain outside and a mordant wind blowing through dripping dark trees. He shivered and growled, unsheathing his claws, but this was not an enemy he could destroy. The day and the night dragged by in misery.

Tigers had been adaptable beasts in the old days, he recalled; they had ranged as far north as Siberia. But his original had been from the tropics. *Hell!* he cursed, and the thunderous roar rattled through the woods.

But then came crisp, clear days with a wild

wind hallooing through a high, pale sky, dead leaves whirling on the gusts and laughing in their thin, dry way. Geese honked in the heavens, southward bound, and the bellowing of stags filled the nights. There was a drunkenness in the air; the tiger rolled in the grass and purred like muted thunder and yowled at the huge orange moon as it rose. His fur thickened, he didn't feel the chill except as a keen tingling in his blood. All his senses were sharpened now, he lived with a knife-edged alertness and learned how to go through the fallen leaves like another shadow.

Indian summer, long lazy days, like a resurrected springtime, enormous stars, the crisp smell of rotting vegetation, and his human mind remembered that the leaves were like gold and bronze and flame. He fished in the brooks, scooping up his prey with one hooked sweep; he ranged the woods and reared on the high ridges under the moon.

Then the rains returned, gray and cold and sodden, the world drowned in a wet woe. At night there was frost, numbing his feet and glittering in the starlight and through the chill silence he could hear the distant beat of the sea. It grew harder to stalk game, he was often hungry. But now he didn't mind that too much, but his reason worried about winter. Maybe he'd better get back.

One night the first snow fell, and in the morning the world was white and still. He plowed through it, growling his anger, and wondered about moving south. But cats aren't given to long journeys. He remembered vaguely that Avi could give him food and shelter.

Avi— For a moment, when he tried to think of her, he thought of a golden, dark-striped body and a harsh feline smell filling the cave above the old wide river. He shook his massive head, angry with himself and the world, and tried to call up her image. The face was dim in his mind, but the scent came back to him, and the low, lovely music of her laughter. He would go to Avi.

He went through the bare forest with the haughty gait of its king, and presently he stood on the beach. The sea was gray and cold and enormous, roaring white-maned on the shore; flying spin-drift stung his eyes. He padded along the strand until he saw her house.

It was oddly silent. He went in through the garden. The door stood open, but there was only desertion inside.

Maybe she was away. He curled up on the floor and went to sleep.

He woke much later, hunger gnawing in his guts, and still no one had come. He recalled that she had been wont to go south for the winter. But she wouldn't have forgotten him, she'd have been back from time to time— But the house had little scent of her, she had been away for a long while. And it was disordered. Had she left hastily?

He went over to the counter. He couldn't remember how it worked, but he did recall the process of dialing and switching. He pulled the lever at random with a paw. Nothing happened.

Nothing! The creator was inert.

He roared his disappointment. Slow, puzzled fear came to him. This wasn't as it should be.

But he was hungry. He'd have to try to get his own food, then, and come back later in hopes of finding Avi. He went back into the woods.

Presently he smelled life under the snow. Bear. Previously, he and the bears had been in a state of watchful neutrality. But this one was asleep, unwary, and his belly cried for food. He tore the shelter apart with a few powerful motions and flung himself on the animal.

It is dangerous to wake a hibernating bear. This one came to with a start, his heavy paw lashed out and the tiger sprang back with blood streaming down his muzzle.

Madness came, a berserk rage that sent him leaping forward. The bear snarled and braced himself. They closed, and suddenly the tiger was fighting for his very life.

He never remembered that battle save as a red whirl of shock and fury, tumbling in the snow and spilling blood to steam in the cold air. Strike, bite, rip, thundering blows against his ribs and skull, the taste of blood hot in his mouth and the insanity of death shrieking and gibbering in his head!

In the end, he staggered bloodily and collapsed on the bear's ripped corpse. For a long time he lay there, and the wild dogs hovered near, waiting for him to die.

After a while he stirred weakly and ate of the bear's flesh. But he couldn't leave. His body was one vast pain, his feet wobbled under him, one paw had been crushed by the great jaws. He lay by the dead bear under the tumbled shelter, and snow fell slowly on them.

The battle and the agony and the nearness of

death brought his old instincts to the fore. All tiger, he licked his tattered form and gulped hunks of rotting meat as the days went by and waited for a measure of health to return.

In the end, he limped back toward his cave. Dreamlike memories nagged him; there had been a house and someone who was good but—but—

He was cold and lame and hungry. Winter had come.

"We have no further use for you," said Felgi, "but in view of the help you've been, you'll be allowed to live—at least till we get back to Procyon and the Council decides your case. Also, you probably have more valuable information about the Solar System than our other prisoners. They're mostly women."

Ramacan looked at the hard, exultant face and answered dully, "If I'd known what you were planning, I'd never have helped."

"Oh, yes, you would have," snorted Felgi. "I saw your reactions when we showed you some of our means of persuasion. You Earthlings are all alike. You've been hiding from death so long that the backbone has all gone out of you. That alone makes you unfit to hold your planet."

"You have the plans of the duplicators and the transmitters and power-beams—all our technology. I helped you get them from the Stations. What more do you want?"

"Earth."

"But why? With the creators and transmitters, you can make your planets like all the old dreams of paradise. Earth is more congenial, yes, but what does environment matter to you now?"

"Earth is still the true home of man," said Felgi. There was a fanaticism in his eyes such as Ramacan had never seen even in nightmare. "It should belong to the best race of man. Also—well, our culture couldn't stand that technology. Procyonite civilization grew up in adversity, it's been nothing but struggle and hardship, it's become part of our nature now. With the Czernigi destroyed, we *must* find another enemy."

Oh yes, thought Ramacan. *It's happened before, in Earth's bloody old past. Nations that knew nothing but war and suffering, became molded by them, glorified the harsh virtues that had enabled them to survive. A militaristic state can't afford peace and leisure and prosperity; its people might begin to think for themselves. So the government looks for conquest outside the borders— Needful or not, there must be war to maintain the control of the military.*

How human are the Procyonites now? What's twisted them in the centuries of their terrible evolution? They're no longer men, they're fighting robots, beasts of prey, they have to have blood.

"You saw us shell the Stations from space," said Felgi. "Rebirth, Creator, Transmitter—they're radioactive craters now. Not a machine is running on Earth, not a tube is alight—nothing! And with the creators on which their lives depended inert, Earthlings will go back to utter savagery."

"Now what?" asked Ramacan wearily.

"We're standing off Mercury, refueling," said Felgi. "Then it's back to Procyon. We'll use our creator to record most of the crew, they can take turns being briefly recreated during the voyage to maintain the ship and correct the course. We'll be little older when we get home.

"Then, of course, the Council will send out a fleet with recorded crews. They'll take over Sol, eliminate the surviving population, and recolonize Earth. After that—" The mad fires blazed high in his eyes. "The stars! A galactic empire, ultimately."

"Just so you can have war," said Ramacan tonelessly. "Just so you can keep your people stupid slaves."

"That's enough," snapped Felgi. "A decadent culture can't be expected to understand our motives."

Ramacan stood thinking. There would still be humans around when the Procyonites came back. There would be forty years to prepare. Men in spaceships, here and there throughout the System, would come home, would see the ruin of Earth and know who must be guilty. With creators, they could rebuild quickly, they could arm themselves, duplicate vengeance-hungry men by the millions.

Unless Solarian man was so far gone in decay that he was only capable of blind panic. But Ramacan didn't think so. Earth had slipped, but not that far.

Felgi seemed to read his mind. There was cruel satisfaction in his tones: "Earth will have no chance to rearm. We're using the power from Mercury Station to run our own large duplicator, turning rock into osmium fuel for our engines. But when we're finished, we'll blow up the Station, too. Spaceships will drift powerless, the colonists on the planets will die as their environmental regulators stop functioning, no wheel will turn in all the Solar System. That, I should think, will be the final touch!"

Indeed, indeed. Without power, without tools, without food or shelter, the final collapse would come. Nothing but a few starveling savages would be left when the Procyonites returned. Ramacan felt an emptiness within himself.

Life had become madness and nightmare. The end. . . .

"You'll stay here till we get around to recording you," said Felgi. He turned on his heel and walked out.

Ramacan slumped back into a seat. His desperate eyes traveled around and around the bare little cabin that was his prison, around and around like the crazy whirl of his thoughts. He looked at the guard who stood in the doorway, leaning on his blaster, contemptuously bored with the captive. If—if— O almighty gods, if *that* was to inherit green Earth!

What to do, what to do? There must be some answer, some way, no problem was altogether without solution. Or was it? What guarantee did he have of cosmic justice? He buried his face in his hands.

I was a coward, he thought. *I was afraid of pain. So I rationalized, I told myself they probably didn't want much, I used my influence to help them get duplicators and plans. And the others were cowards too, they yielded, they were cravenly eager to help the conquerors—and this is our pay!*

What to do, what to do? If somehow the ship were lost, if it never came back— The Procyonites would wonder. They'd send another ship or two—no more—to investigate. And in forty years Sol could be ready to meet those ships—ready to carry the war to an unprepared enemy—if in the meantime they'd had a chance to rebuild, if Mercury Power Station was spared—

But the ship would blow the Station out of existence, and the ship would return with news of Sol's ruin, and the invaders would come swarming in—would go ravening out through an unsuspecting galaxy like a spreading plague—

How to stop the ship—*now?*

Ramacan grew aware of the thudding of his heart; it seemed to shake his whole body with its violence. And his hands were cold and clumsy, his mouth was parched, he was afraid.

He got up and walked over toward the guard. The Procyonite hefted his blaster, but there was no alertness in him, he had no fear of an unarmed member of the conquered race.

He'll shoot me down, thought Ramacan. *The death I've been running from all my life is on me now. But it's been a long life and a good one, and better to finish it now than drag out a few miserable years as their despised prisoner, and—and—I hate their guts!*

"What do you want?" asked the Procyonite.

"I feel sick," said Ramacan. His voice was almost a whisper in the dryness of his throat. "Let me out."

"Get back."

"It'll be messy. Let me go to the lavatory."

He stumbled, nearly falling. "Go ahead," said the guard curtly. "I'll be along, remember."

Ramacan swayed on his feet as he approached the man. His shaking hands closed on the blaster barrel and yanked the weapon loose. Before the guard could yell, Ramacan drove the butt into his face. A remote corner of his mind was shocked at the savagery that welled up in him when the bones crunched.

The guard toppled. Ramacan eased him to the floor, slugged him again to make sure he would lie quiet, and stripped him of his long outer coat, his boots, and helmet. His hands were really trembling now; he could hardly get the simple garments on.

If he was caught—well, it only made a few minutes' difference. But he was still afraid. Fear screamed inside him.

He forced himself to walk with nightmare slowness down the long corridor. Once he passed another man, but there was no discovery. When he had rounded the corner, he was violently sick.

He went down a ladder to the engine room. Thank the gods he'd been interested enough to inquire about the layout of the ship when they first arrived! The door stood open and he went in.

A couple of engineers were watching the giant creator at work. It pulsed and hummed and throbbed with power, energy from the sun and from dissolving atoms of rocks—atoms recreated as the osmium that would power the ship's engines on the long voyage back. Tons of fuel spilling down into the bins.

Ramacan closed the soundproof door and shot the engineers.

Then he went over to the creator and reset the controls. It began to manufacture plutonium.

He smiled then, with an immense relief, an incredulous realization that he had won. He sat down and cried with sheer joy.

The ship would not get back. Mercury Station would endure. And on that basis, a few determined men in the Solar System could rebuild. There would be horror on Earth, howling chaos, most of its population would plunge into savagery and death. But enough would live, and remain civilized, and get ready for revenge.

Maybe it was for the best, he thought. Maybe Earth really had gone into a twilight of purposeless ease. True it was that there had been none of the old striving and hoping and gallantry which had made man what he was. No art, no science, no adventure—a smug self-satisfaction, an unreal immortality in a synthetic paradise. Maybe this shock and challenge was what Earth needed, to show the starward way again.

As for him, he had had many centuries of life, and he realized now what a deep inward weariness there had been in him. *Death*, he thought, *death is the longest voyage of all. Without death there is no evolution, no real meaning to life, the ultimate adventure has been snatched away*.

There had been a girl once, he remembered, and she had died before the rebirth machines became available. Odd—after all these centuries he could still remember how her hair had rippled in the wind, one day on a high summery hill. He wondered if he would see her.

He never felt the explosion as the plutonium reached critical mass.

Avi's feet were bleeding. Her shoes had finally given out, and rocks and twigs tore at her feet. The snow was dappled with blood.

Weariness clawed at her, she couldn't keep going—but she had to, she had to, she was afraid to stop in the wilderness.

She had never been alone in her life. There had always been the televisors and the transmitters, no place on Earth had been more than an instant away. But the world had expanded into immensity, the machines were dead, there was only cold and gloom and empty white distances. The world of warmth and music and laughter and casual enjoyment was as remote and unreal as a dream.

Was it a dream? Had she always stumbled sick and hungry through a nightmare world of leafless trees and drifting snow and wind that sheathed her in cold through the thin rags of her garments? Or was this the dream, a sudden madness of horror and death?

Death—no, no, no, she couldn't die, she was one of the immortals, she mustn't die!

The wind blew and blew.

Night was falling, winter night. A wild dog bayed, somewhere out in the gloom. She tried to scream, but her throat was raw with shrieking, only a dry croak would come out.

Help me, help me, help me.

Maybe she should have stayed with the man. He had devised traps, had caught an occasional rabbit or squirrel and flung her the leavings. But he looked at her so strangely when several days had gone by without a catch. He would have killed her and eaten her; she had to flee.

Run, run, run— She couldn't run, the forest reached on forever, she was caught in cold and night, hunger and death.

What had happened, what had happened, what had become of the world? What would become of her?

She had liked to pretend she was one of the ancient goddesses, creating what she willed out of nothingness, served by a huge and eternal world whose one purpose was to serve her. Where was that world now?

Hunger twisted in her like a knife. She tripped over a snow-buried log and lay there, trying feebly to rise.

We were too soft, too complacent, she thought dimly. *We lost all our powers, we were just little parasites on our machines. Now we're unfit—*

No! I won't have it! I was a goddess once—

Spoiled brat, jeered the demon in her mind. *Baby crying for its mother. You should be old enough to look after yourself—after all these centuries. You shouldn't be running in circles waiting for a help that will never come, you should be helping yourself, making a shelter, finding nuts and roots, building a trap. But you can't. All the self-reliance has withered out of you.*

No—help, help, help—

Something moved in the gloom. She choked a scream. Yellow eyes glowed like twin fires, and the immense form stepped noiselessly forth.

For an instant she gibbered in a madness of

fear, and then sudden realization came and left her gaping with unbelief—then instant eager acceptance.

There could only be one tiger in this forest.

"Harol," she whispered, and climbed to her feet. "Harol."

It was all right. The nightmare was over. Harol would look after her. He would hunt for her, protect her, bring her back to the world of machines that *must* still exist. "Harol," she cried. "Harol, my dear—"

The tiger stood motionless; only his twitching tail had life. Briefly, irrelevantly, remembered sounds trickled through his mind: *"Your basic mentality should be stable for a year or two, barring accidents. . . ."* But the noise was meaningless, it slipped through his brain into oblivion.

He was hungry. The crippled paw hadn't healed well, he couldn't catch game.

Hunger, the most eternal need of all, grinding within him, filling his tiger brain and tiger body until nothing else was left.

He stood looking at the thing that didn't run away. He had killed another a while back—he licked his mouth at the thought.

From somewhere long ago he remembered that the thing had once been—he had been—he couldn't remember—

He stalked forward.

"Harol," said Avi. There was fear rising horribly in her voice.

The tiger stopped. He knew that voice. He remembered—he remembered—

He had known her once. There was something about her that held him back.

But he was hungry. And his instincts were clamoring in him.

But if only he could remember, before it was too late—

Time stretched into a horrible eternity while they stood facing each other—the lady and the tiger.

THE DISINTEGRATING SKY

liff Bronson's apartment was very like himself. It
as furnished in quiet good taste, a little archaic
its heavy dark furniture and the fireplace, where
nall flames sputtered and sang and beat ruddy
ts against the soft lamplight. There were shelves
 records, the old masters of music, and the walls
ere lined with well-worn copies of the world's
eat literature, from Aeschylus to Guthrie.

But among the records were also to be found
e sinister discords of Stravinsky and Berlioz along
ith the latest better popular releases. And some
ery curious and disquieting volumes nestled
nongst Shakespeare and Goethe and Voltaire.
cross the room Frans Hals' sardonic Jester leered
 a recent Dali. The arrangement seemed delib-
ate, perhaps symbolic.

There was a broad window looking down the

precipitous wall to the million winking blazing
lights of New York. Reality surfed its remote thun
der against the room. But within its walls the
urgent and immediate were lost. The costly radio
television was turned off. Its voice could not blare
of the latest step toward a war that now could only
be weeks or days away. Its speaker breathed out
the languid recorded tones of Delius, rest and
forgetfulness beside drowsy streams, a pastoral peace
that had perhaps never really existed.

Not the least advantage of Bronson's comfortable bachelorhood was the freedom to hold all-
night conversation with those he found interesting.
He liked to bring together minds as diverse as he
could locate and let them clash over whisky and
cigars, while he remained the amused host-spectator
with only an occasional carefully polished inter-
jection.

Tonight he had invited Raymond Burkhardt and
Carl Gray. There was also a new acqaintance of
his, Bernie Cogswell, but he was proving a disappointment. He slumped in a deep chair, clutching
his glass as a child might grip its mother's hand,
saying little more than politeness required. The
eyes were haunted in his haggard young face.

Bronson had hoped that Cogswell might tell
them a little of the latest nuclear bomb project
with which, as a physicist, he had a minor associa-
tion. At the very least he might have applied some
good positivistic philosophy to the present argu-
ment. But no such luck.

However, Burkhardt and Gray were making up
for it. They had drifted into a debate which was
delightfully remote from the urgencies of the pres-

ent, and their words were the very images of their minds. They were two mutually alien human types who had locked horns and would never conceivably reach agreement.

Gray was an executive in one of the larger manufacturing corporations, hard-headed, a stickler for facts—but he was not without imagination, was the only conservative Bronson could recall meeting who could make a really good case for his side.

Burkhardt was a sculptor, mildly prosperous since his weird creations had begun enjoying a certain vogue—a dreamer, a poet, an avowed mystic—yet well versed in the logical method which he professed to scorn.

Bronson felt a little like a playwright—or, better, a novelist on the order of Thomas Mann, selecting his characters from absolute types and then setting them free to argue it out. With occasional steering from himself, of course. Now if only Cogswell would be a little more cooperative . . .

"But how do you *know?*" Gray insisted. "How can you prove it?"

"How do you know you're sitting in a chair and not in the arms of an octopus? Prove that," replied Burkhardt.

"Well—I can see that, feel it . . ."

"Right! You use your senses. You experience the chair directly. In the same way I experienced his knowledge directly."

"But look here. We're all sane and reasonable men—I think. We'll all agree that this is a chair. But since nobody will agree with you, since nobody claims to have had the same experience, isn't

it more reasonable to suppose it purely sub-
jective—a dream, an hallucination?"

"Suppose I were the only man in the world with
eyes. Would you then claim that light and color
were no more than mere hallucinations of mine?"

"There would be ways to check on it, just as we
can check the existence of radio waves without
being able to see them. But how can anyone check
on your statement that we're all merely characters
in a book?"

"By having the same experience. By opening
your eyes. Anyway, I didn't claim we were all
characters of some supercosmic author. That's an
oversimplification."

"Isn't your idea essentially Berkeleyan?" suggested Bronson. "Aren't you claiming that all reality exists only as a perception or thought in the
mind of God?"

"Not that either," said Burkhardt. "It—it's hard
to put into words. It came on me all at once, in
that dreamy half-reverie just before you fall asleep.
I had been reading Berkeley, yes, and suppose
that's what triggered this in my mind. But it is
something different."

" 'It's all my own invention,' " murmured Bronson.

"I was wondering about the flow of time," said
Burkhardt. "Why do we all perceive time as flowing in the same direction? What becomes of the
past? What is the future and why can't we know it
as we know the past? Simply because it doesn't
exist yet?"

"Seems like a scientific question," said Bronson.
"What do you think about it, Bernie?"

"Eh?" Cogswell stirred and blinked abstractedly at them. "Pardon me, I didn't quite get the gist of the last remark."

"What's the nature of time?"

"Why—nobody really knows. According to relativity, of course, time is simply one dimension in a four-dimensional continuum. The past and the future are equally real and fixed. But of course wave-mechanics and the uncertainty principle may throw a little doubt on that theory."

"Why do we see time as flowing instead of static?" asked Gray.

Cogswell shrugged. "Who knows? We just do. Some authorities have suggested that the time-direction is the direction of increase of entropy. But somehow I've never been satisfied with that theory, perhaps because it's so vague."

Burkhardt looked triumphant. "I say we move from past to future because the Author is writing all the time. The movement of time is the movement of—of his pen, to make a very crude analogy. The future has not yet been written. The present is what he's writing this instant. The past is what he has already written."

"And he never rewrites," said Bronson with a wry smile. " '*The moving finger writes, and having writ . . .* ' "

"If he does rewrite," said Gray with the air of a man descending to a child's make-believe, "in the very nature of the case we'd never know it." Then, a little angrily, "But that's all nonsense. You're saying we aren't real, that we're just figments of some enormous being's imagination. But damn it, I *know* I'm real. As you'd say, Burkhardt, it's a matter of direct experience."

"Of course it is," said Burkhardt patiently. "I'm not denying that we're real. I'm simply explaining *how* we are. This table isn't less heavy because science has shown that it's built up of atoms which are mostly empty space. The heaviness has been explained, not explained away. That's all I'm trying to do with reality."

"Then everything is being written by a great Author—but who's going to read it?" asked Gray.

"Wait a minute," said Bronson. The fantasy amused him—he wanted to carry it to its logical conclusion. "Who said that all the universe is the work of one writer? It looks more reasonable to me that each inhabited planet—and there must be many of them in the cosmos—is the work of one of these creatures.

"Then there'd be a lot of them, you see, some of which aren't authors and can pay in whatever unimaginable currency they have to see what the writers have done. This is the Book of Earth. There must be many other novels."

"What about planets without intelligent life?" snorted Gray.

"Oh, call them the scrawlings of children. Later on, as they grow up, they'll be able to do characterization." Bronson looked into his empty glass and got up. "Who wants another shot?"

There was a moment while whisky and soda were being poured and the men resettled themselves. The fire burned low on the hearth, little ghosts of flame dancing among the cinders. Outside the window the night flared and glittered.

"In a way it's a comforting thought," said Gray. "It would mean that something greater and wiser than ourselves was in existence, a higher order of reality, which will go on forever, whatever may happen to us. But it's damned hard on the human ego. Makes us seem so very futile."

"You realize, of course," said Burkhardt, "that it's the Author who's putting those thoughts in your head."

"I certainly do not," snapped Gray. "Hell, if Earth were a book things would happen a lot more sensibly than they really do."

Bronson smiled again and blew smoke rings. "Not necessarily," he said. "We've got a very young writer. He doesn't know the first thing about the principles of literature. The majority of his characters are dull and stupid. He doesn't have a plot, just a long meaningless narrative broken by melodramatic catastrophes.

"The few really great events lead merely to piddling anticlimaxes—with no feeling whatsoever for the dramatic unities. Earth's history reads like the magnum opus of a romantic fourteen-year-old."

"I hope everything he ever writes is rejected," muttered Cogswell with bitterness.

"I don't think so," said Burkhardt. "He has elements of genius. Once in a while he'll come up with a character or a situation that is absolutely sublime—a Christ, a Shakespeare, a Beethoven, an Einstein, the discovery of fire or of America. Oh, he'll go far when he's mastered his technique. He's just starting. Give him time."

"Time to write some other planet, maybe," said

Cogswell. "But *we're* the early effort, the botched manuscript. I think he's tired of us."

They looked at him with something of the layman's superstitious awe for the Scientist with a capital S. Cogswell was a little drunk. His smile was crooked and an unruly forelock flopped over his moist skin toward haggard eyes.

"I'm not supposed to know this," he said with the slow precision of intoxication. "I'm just a very little shot on the project, not big enough to rate a guard or a gag. But things leak out here and there, tiny pieces of information that can be put together if you know how.

"And, brethren, the total-disintegration bomb is no longer a theory. It has been built. We're making dozens. And *they* are too."

There was a long moment of a silence that thrummed like a dynamo. Bronson scowled. He hated to be reminded of the unpleasantness outside. There were too many reminders these days.

"It's going to be used," said Cogswell. "It's going to be used because neither side will dare stand by in the fear that the other will cut loose all at once. And just what happens when matter is converted one hundred percent into energy by the ton— nobody knows. My guess is that it will touch off disintegration in the earth's crust. I made some calculations . . ."

Bronson got up and walked over to the window. He stood looking down at the hectic night. His smile was a desperate attempt at restoring the broken mood of gay unreality. "It will at least be a spectacular way to go out," he said.

"Sure!" Cogswell's laugh was brittle. "The most

melodramatic way you can imagine. Isn't it just the way your adolescent Author would choose? To hell with winding up all the million loose ends in a story that has begun to bore him. Wipe 'em all out, let every blasted one of his characters go up in flame, start on something more interesting!"

Sweat gleamed suddenly on Bronson's face. "You know," he said, "you know, if I'd written such a book back in my teens and got fed up with it, I would have taken a few of my characters just before the end and made them realize what they were—characters in a poorly-written novel, out of my own mind.

"It would have been my way of expressing my disgust with their mechanicalness, their unrealness, their unsatisfactoriness. And then I'd have written a flaming finis."

They stared at him and he stood looking out the window. Faraway and faintly the scream of sirens came to him and the lights started to go out. He saw rocket flames cut their fiery trails across the disintegrating sky.

AMONG THIEVES

His Excellency M'Katze Unduma, Ambassador of the Terrestrial Federation to the Double Kingdom, was not accustomed to being kept waiting. But as the minutes dragged into an hour, anger faded before a chill deduction.

In this bleakly clock-bound society a short delay was bad manners, even if it were unintentional. But if you kept a man of rank cooling his heels for an entire sixty minutes, you offered him an unforgivable insult. Rusch was a barbarian, but he was too canny to humiliate Earth's representative without reason.

Which bore out everything that Terrestrial Intelligence had discovered. From a drunken junior officer, weeping in his cups because Old Earth, Civilization, was going to be attacked and the campus where he had once learned and loved would be scorched to ruin by *his* fire guns—to the battle plans and annotations thereon, which six men had died to smuggle out of the Royal War College— and now, this degradation of the ambassador himself—everything fitted.

The Margrave of Drakenstane had sold out Civilization.

Unduma shuddered, beneath the iridescent cloak, embroidered robe, and ostrich-plume headdress of his rank. He swept the antechamber with the eyes of a trapped animal.

This castle was ancient, dating back some eight hundred years to the first settlement of Norstad. The grim square massiveness of it, fused stone piled into a turreted mountain, was not much relieved by modern fittings. Tableservs, loungers, drapes, jewel mosaics, and biomurals only clashed with those fortress walls and ringing flagstones; fluorosheets did not light up all the dark corners, there was perpetual dusk up among the rafters where the old battle banners hung.

A dozen guards were posted around the room, in breastplate and plumed helmet but with very modern blast rifles. They were identical seven-foot blends, and none of them moved at all, you couldn't even see them breathe. It was an unnerving sight for a Civilized man.

Unduma stubbed out his cigar, swore miserably to himself, and wished he had at least brought along a book.

The inner door opened on noiseless hinges and a shavepate officer emerged. He clicked his heels and bowed at Unduma. "His Lordship will be honored to receive you now, excellency."

The ambassador throttled his anger, nodded, and stood up. He was a tall thin man, the relatively light skin and sharp features of Bantu stock predominant in him. Earth's emissaries were normally chosen to approximate a local ideal of beauty—hard to do for some of those weird little cultures scattered through the galaxy—and Norstad-Ostarik had been settled by a rather extreme Caucasoid type which had almost entirely emigrated from the home planet.

The aide showed him through the door and disappeared. Hans von Thoma Rusch, Margrave of Drakenstane, Lawman of the Western Folkmote, Hereditary Guardian on the White River Gates, et cetera, et cetera, et cetera, sat waiting behind a desk at the end of an enormous black-and-red tile floor. He had a book in his hands, and didn't close it till Unduma, sandals whispering on the great chessboard squares, had come near. Then he stood up and made a short ironic bow.

"How do you do, your excellency," he said. "I am sorry to be so late. Please sit." Such curtness was no apology at all, and both of them knew it.

Unduma lowered himself to a chair in front of the desk. He would *not* show temper, he thought, he was here for a greater purpose. His teeth clamped together.

"Thank you, your lordship," he said tonelessly. "I hope you will have time to talk with me in some detail. I have come on a matter of grave importance."

Rusch's right eyebrow tilted up, so that the archaic monocle he affected beneath it seemed in danger of falling out. He was a big man, stiffly and solidly built, yellow hair cropped to a wiry brush around the long skull, a scar puckering his left cheek. He wore Army uniform, the gray high-collared tunic and old-fashioned breeches and shiny boots of his planet; the trident and suns of a primary general; a sidearm, its handle worn smooth from much use. If ever the iron barbarian with the iron brain had an epitome, thought Unduma, here he sat!

"Well, your excellency," murmured Rusch—though the harsh Norron language did not lend itself to murmurs—"of course I'll be glad to hear you out. But after all, I've no standing in the Ministry, except as unofficial advisor, and—"

"Please," Unduma lifted a hand. "Must we keep up the fable? You not only speak for all the landed warloads—and the Nor-Samurai are still the most powerful single class in the Double Kingdom—but you have the General Staff in your pouch and, ah, you are well thought of by the royal family. I think I can talk directly to you."

Rusch did not smile, but neither did he trouble to deny what everyone knew, that he was the leader of the fighting aristocracy, friend of the widowed Queen Regent, virtual step-father of her eight-year-old son King Hjalmar—in a word, that he was the dictator. If he preferred to keep a small title and not have his name unnecessarily before the public, what difference did that make?

"I'll be glad to pass on whatever you wish to say to the proper authorities," he answered slowly. "Pipe." That was an order to his chair, which produced a lit briar for him.

Unduma felt appalled. This series of—informalities—was like one savage blow after another. Till now, in the three hundred-year history of relations between Earth and the Double Kingdom, the Terrestrial ambassador had ranked everyone but God and the royal family.

No human planet, no matter how long sundered from the main stream, no matter what strange ways it had wandered, failed to remember that Earth was Earth, the home of man and the heart of Civilization. No *human* planet—had Norstad-Ostarik, then, gone the way of Kolresh?

Biologically, no, thought Unduma with an inward shudder. Not culturally—yet. But it shrieked at him, from every insolent movement and twist of words, that Rusch had made a political deal.

"Well?" said the Margrave.

Unduma cleared his throat desperately, and leaned forward. "Your lordship," he said, "my embassy cannot help taking notice of certain public statements, as well as certain military preparations and other matters of common knowledge—"

"And items your spies have dug up," drawled Rusch.

Unduma started. "My lord!"

"My good ambassador," grinned Rusch, "it was you who suggested a straightforward talk. I know Earth has spies here. In any event, it's impossible to hide so large a business as the mobilization of two planets for war."

Unduma felt sweat trickle down his ribs.

"There is . . . you . . . your Ministry has only announced it is a . . . a defense measure," he stammered. "I had hoped . . . frankly, yes, till the last minute I hoped you . . . your people might see fit to join us against Kolresh."

There was a moment's quiet. *So* quiet, thought Unduma. A redness crept up Rusch's cheeks, the scar stood livid and his pale eyes were the coldest thing Unduma had ever seen.

Then, slowly, the Margrave got it out through his teeth: "For a number of centuries, your excellency, our people hoped Earth might join them."

"What do you mean?" Unduma forgot all polished inanities. Rusch didn't seem to notice. He stood up and went to the window.

"Come here," he said. "Let me show you something."

The window was a modern inset of a clear, invisible plastic, a broad sheet high in the castle's infamous Witch Tower. It looked out on a black sky, the sun was down and the glacial forty-hour darkness of northern Norstad was crawling toward midnight.

Stars glittered mercilessly keen in an emptiness which seemed like crystal, which seemed about to ring thinly in contracting anguish under the cold. Ostarik, the companion planet, stood low to the south, a gibbous moon of steely blue; it never moved in that sky, the two worlds forever faced each other, the windy white peaks of one glaring at the warm lazy seas of the other. Northward, a great curtain of aurora flapped halfway around the cragged horizon.

From this dizzy height, Unduma could see little of the town Drakenstane: a few high-peaked roofs and small glowing windows, lamps lonesome above frozen streets. There wasn't much to see anyhow—no big cities on either planet, only the small towns which had grown from scattered thorps, each clustered humbly about the manor of its lord. Beyond lay winter fields, climbing up the valley walls to the hard green blink of glaciers. It must be blowing out there; he saw snowdevils chase ghostly across the blue-tinged desolation.

Rusch spoke roughly: "Not much of a planet we've got here, is it? Out on the far end of nowhere, a thousand light-years from your precious Earth, and right in the middle of a glacial epoch. Have you ever wondered why we don't set up weather-control stations and give this world a decent climate?"

"Well," began Unduma, "of course, the exigencies of—"

"Of war." Rusch sent his hand upward in a chopping motion, to sweep around the alien constellations. Among them burned Polaris, less than thirty parsecs away, huge and cruelly bright. "We never had a chance. Every time we thought we could begin, there would be war, usually with Kolresh, and the labor and materials would have to go for that. Once, about two centuries back, we did actually get stations established, it was even beginning to warm up a little. Kolresh blasted them off the map.

"Norstad was settled eight hundred years ago. For seven of those centuries, we've had Kolresh at our throats. Do you wonder if we've grown tired?"

"My lord, I . . . I can sympathize," said Unduma awkwardly. "I am not ignorant of your heroic history. But it would seem to me . . . after all, Earth has also fought—"

"At a range of a thousand light-years!" jeered

Rusch. "The forgotten war. A few underpaid patrolmen in obsolete rustbucket ships to defend unimportant outposts from sporadic Kolreshite raids. We live on their borders!"

"It would certainly appear, your lordship, that Kolresh is your natural enemy," said Unduma. "As indeed it is of all Civilization, of Homo sapiens himself. What I cannot credit are the, ah, the rumors of an, er, alliance—"

"And why shouldn't we?" snarled Rusch. "For seven hundred years we've held them at bay, while your precious so-called Civilization grew fat behind a wall of our dead young men. The temptation to recoup some of our losses by helping Kolresh conquer Earth is very strong!"

"You don't mean it!" The breath rushed from Unduma's lungs.

The other man's face was like carved bone. "Don't jump to conclusions," he answered. "I merely point out that from our side there's a good deal to be said for such a policy. Now if Earth is prepared to make a different policy worth our while—do you understand? Nothing is going to happen in the immediate future. You have time to think about it."

"I would have to . . . communicate with my government," whispered Unduma.

"Of course," said Rusch. His bootheels clacked on the floor as he went back to his desk. "I've had a memorandum prepared for you, an unofficial informal sort of protocol, points which his majesty's government would like to make the basis of negotiations with the Terrestrial Federation. Ah, here!" He picked up a bulky folio. "I suggest you take a leave of absence, your excellency, go home and show your superiors this, ah—"

"Ultimatum," said Unduma in a sick voice.

Rusch shrugged. "Call it what you will." His tone was empty and remote, as if he had already cut himself and his people out of Civilization.

As he accepted the folio, Unduma noticed the book beside it, the one Rusch had been reading: a local edition of Schakspier, badly printed on sleazy paper, but in the original Old Anglic. Odd thing for a barbarian dictator to read. But then, Rusch was a bit of an historical scholar, as well as an enthusiastic kayak racer, meteor polo player, chess champion, mountain climber, and . . . and all-around scoundrel!

Norstad lay in the grip of a ten-thousand-year winter, while Ostarik was a heaven of blue seas breaking on warm island sands. Nevertheless, because Ostarik harbored a peculiarly nasty plague virus, it remained an unattainable paradise in the sky till a bare two hundred fifty years ago. Then a research team from Earth got to work, found an effective vaccine, and saw a mountain carved into their likeness by the Norron folk.

It was through such means—and the sheer weight of example, the liberty and wealth and happiness of its people—that the Civilization centered on Earth had been propagating itself among colonies isolated for centuries. There were none which lacked reverence for Earth the Mother, Earth the Wise, Earth the Kindly: none but Kolresh, which had long ceased to be human.

Rusch's private speedster whipped him from the

icicle walls of Festning Drakenstane to the rose
gardens of Sorgenlos in an hour of hell-bat haste
across vacuum. But it was several hours more until
he and the queen could get away from their cour-
tiers and be alone.

They walked through geometric beds of smoldering blooms, under songbirds and fronded trees,
while the copper spires of the little palace reached
up to the evening star and the hours-long sunset of
Ostarik blazed gold across great quiet waters. The
island was no more than a royal retreat, but lately
it had known agonies.

Queen Ingra stooped over a mutant rose, tiger
striped and a foot across; she plucked the petals
from it and said close to weeping: "But I liked
Unduma. I don't want him to hate us."

"He's not a bad sort," agreed Rusch. He stood
behind her in a black dress uniform with silver
insignia, like a formal version of death.

"He's more than that, Hans. He stands for
decency—Norstad froze our souls, and Ostarik hasn't
thawed them. I thought Earth might—" Her voice
trailed off. She was slender and dark, still young,
and her folk came from the rainy dales of Norstad's
equator, a farm race with gentler ways than the
miners and fishermen and hunters of the red-
haired ice ape who had bred Rusch. In her throat,
the Norron language softened to a burning music;
the Drakenstane men spat their words out rough-
edged.

"Earth might what?" Rusch turned a moody gaze
to the west. "Lavish more gifts on us? We were
always proud of paying our own way."

"Oh, no," said Ingra wearily. "After all, we could

trade with them, furs and minerals and so on, if ninety per cent of our production didn't have to go into defense. I only thought they might teach us how to be human."

"I had assumed we were still classified Homo sapiens," said Rusch in a parched tone.

"Oh, you know what I mean!" She turned on him, violet eyes suddenly aflare. "Sometimes I wonder if *you're* human, Margrave Hans von Thoma Rusch. I mean free, free to be something more than a robot, free to raise children knowing they won't have their lungs shoved out their mouths when a Kolreshite cruiser hulls one of our spaceships. What is our whole culture, Hans? A layer of brutalized farmhands and factory workers—serfs! A top crust of heel-clattering aristocrats who live for nothing but war. A little folk art, folk music, folk saga, full of blood and treachery. Where are our symphonies, novels, cathedrals, research laboratories . . . where are people who can say what they wish and make what they will of their lives and be happy?"

Rusch didn't answer for a moment. He looked at her, unblinking behind his monocle, till she dropped her gaze and twisted her hands together. Then he said only: "You exaggerate."

"Perhaps. It's still the basic truth." Rebellion rode in her voice. "It's what all the other worlds think of us."

"Even if the democratic assumption—that the eternal verities can be discovered by counting enough noses—were true," said Rusch, "you can-

not repeal eight hundred years of history by
decree."

"No. But you could work toward it," she said. "I
think you're wrong in despising the common man,
Hans . . . when was he ever given a chance, in
this kingdom? We could make a beginning now,
and Earth could send psychotechnic advisors, and
in two or three generations—"

"What would Kolresh be doing while we experi-
mented with forms of government?" he laughed.

"Always Kolresh." Her shoulders, slim behind
the burning-red cloak, slumped. "Kolresh turned
a hundred hopeful towns into radioactive craters
and left the gnawed bones of children in the fields.
Kolresh killed my husband, like a score of kings
before him. Kolresh blasted your family to ash, Hans,
and scarred your face and your soul—" She whirled
back on him, fists aloft, and almost screamed: "Do
you want to make an ally of Kolresh?"

The Margrave took out his pipe and began filling it. The saffron sundown, reflected off the ocean
to his face, gave him a metal look.

"Well," he said, "we've been at peace with them
for all of ten years now. Almost a record."

"Can't we find allies? Real ones? I'm sick of
being a figurehead? I'd befriend Ahuramazda, New
Mars, Lagrange— We could raise a crusade against
Kolresh, wipe every last filthy one of them out of
the universe!"

"Now who's a heel-clattering aristocrat?" grinned
Rusch.

He lit his pipe and strolled toward the beach.
She stood for an angry moment, then sighed and
followed him.

"Do you think it hasn't been tried?" he said patiently. "For generations we've tried to build up a permanent alliance directed at Kolresh. What temporary ones we achieved have always fallen apart. Nobody loves us enough—and, since we've always taken the heaviest blows, nobody hates Kolresh enough."

He found a bench on the glistening edge of the strand, and sat down and looked across a steady march of surf, turned to molten gold by the low sun and the incandescent western clouds. Ingra joined him.

"I can't really blame the others for not liking us," she said in a small voice. "We are over-mechanized and undercultured, arrogant, tactless, undemocratic, hard-boiled . . . oh, yes. But their own self-interest—"

"They don't imagine it can happen to them," replied Rusch contemptuously. "And there are even pro-Kolresh elements, here and there." He raised his voice an octave: "Oh, my dear sir, my dear Margrave, what are you *saying?* Why, of *course* Kolresh would never attack us! They made a *treaty* never to attack us!"

Ingra sighed, forlornly. Rusch laid an arm across her shoulders. They sat for a while without speaking.

"Anyway," said the man finally, "Kolresh is too strong for any combination of powers in this part of the galaxy. We and they are the only ones with a military strength worth mentioning. Even Earth would have a hard time defeating them, and Earth, of course, will lean backward before undertaking a major war. She has too much to lose; it's so much

more comfortable to regard the Kolreshite raids as
mere piracies, the skirmishes as 'police actions.'
She just plain will not pay the stiff price of an
army and a navy able to whip Kolresh and occupy
the Kolreshite planets."

"And so it is to be war again." Ingra looked out
in desolation across the sea.

"Maybe not," said Rusch. "Maybe a different
kind of war, at least—no more black ships coming
out of *our* sky."

He blew smoke for a while, as if gathering courage, then spoke in a quick, impersonal manner:
"Look here. We Norrons are not a naval power.
It's not in our tradition. Our navy has always been
inadequate and always will be. But we can breed
the toughest soldiers in the known galaxy, in un-
limited numbers; we can condition them into fighting machines, and equip them with the most lethal
weapons living flesh can wield.

"Kolresh, of course, is just the opposite. Space
nomads, small population, able to destroy anything their guns can reach but not able to dig in
and hold it against us. For seven hundred years,
we and they have been the elephant and the whale.
Neither could ever win a real victory over the
other; war became the normal state of affairs, peace
a breathing spell. Because of the mutation, there
will always be war, as long as one single Kolreshite
lives. We can't kill them, and we can't befriend
them—all we can do is to be bled white to stop
them."

A wind sighed over the slow thunder on the
beach. A line of sea birds crossed the sky, thin and
black against glowing bronze.

"I know," said Ingra. "I know the history, and I know what you're leading up to. Kolresh will furnish transportation and naval escort; Norstad-Ostarik will furnish men. Between us, we may be able to take Earth."

"We will," said Rusch flatly. "Earth has grown plump and lazy. She can't possibly rearm enough in a few months to stop such a combination."

"And all the galaxy will spit on our name."

"All the galaxy will lie open to conquest, once Earth has fallen."

"How long do you think we would last, riding the Kolresh tiger?"

"I have no illusions about them, my dear. But neither can I see any way to break this eternal deadlock. In a fluid situation, such as the collapse of Earth would produce, we might be able to create a navy as good as theirs. They've never yet given us a chance to build one, but perhaps—"

"Perhaps not! I doubt very much it was a meteor which wrecked my husband's ship, five years ago. I think Kolresh knew of his hopes, of the shipyard he wanted to start, and murdered him."

"It's probable," said Rusch.

"And you would league us with them." Ingra turned a colorless face on him. "I'm still the queen. I forbid any further consideration of this . . . this obscene alliance!"

Rusch sighed. "I was afraid of that, your highness." For a moment he looked gray, tired. "You have a veto power, of course. But I don't think the Ministry would continue in office a regent who used it against the best interests of—"

She leaped to her feet. "You wouldn't!"

"Oh, you'd not be harmed," said Rusch with a crooked smile. "Not even deposed. You'd be in protective custody, shall we say. Of course, his majesty, your son, would have to be educated elsewhere, but if you wish—"

Her palm cracked on his face. He made no motion.

"I . . . won't veto—" Ingra shook her head. Then her back grew stiff. "Your ship will be ready to take you home, my lord. I do not think we shall require your presence here again."

"As you will, your highness," mumbled the dictator of the Double Kingdom.

Though he returned with a bitter word in his mouth, Unduma felt the joy, the biological rightness of being home, rise warm within him. He sat on a terrace under the mild sky of Earth, with the dear bright flow of the Zambezi River at his feet and the slim towers of the Capital City rearing as far as he could see, each gracious, in its own green park. The people on the clean quiet streets wore airy blouses and colorful kilts—not the trousers for men, ankle-length skirts for women, which muffled the sad folk of Norstad. And there was educated conversation in the gentle Tierrans language, music from an open window, laughter on the verandahs and children playing in the parks: freedom, law, and leisure.

The thought that this might be rubbed out of history, that the robots of Norstad and the snake-souled monsters of Kolresh might tramp between broken spires where starved Earthmen hid, was a tearing in Unduma.

He managed to lift his drink and lean back with the proper casual elegance. "No, sir," he said, "they are not bluffing."

Ngu Chilongo, Premier of the Federation Parliament, blinked unhappy eyes. He was a small grizzled man, and a wise man, but this lay beyond everything he had known in a long lifetime and he was slow to grasp it.

"But surely—" he began. "Surely this . . . this Rusch person is not insane. He cannot think that his two planets, with a population of, what is it, perhaps one billion, can overcome four billion Terrestrials!"

"There would also be several million Kolreshites to help," reminded Unduma. "However, they would handle the naval end of it entirely—and their navy *is* considerably stronger than ours. The Norron forces would be the ones which actually landed, to fight the air and ground battles. And out of those paltry one billion, Rusch can raise approximately one hundred million soldiers."

Chilongo's glass crashed to the terrace. "What!"

"It's true, sir." The third man present, Mustafa Lefarge, Minister of Defense, spoke in a miserable tone. "It's a question of every able-bodied citizen, male and female, being a trained member of the armed forces. In time of war, virtually everyone not in actual combat is directly contributing to some phase of the effort—a civilian economy virtually ceases to exist. They're used to getting along for years at a stretch with no comforts and a bare minimum of necessities." His voice grew sardonic. "By necessities, they mean things like food and ammunition—not, say, entertainment or cultural activity, as we assume."

"A hundred million," whispered Chilongo. He stared at his hands. "Why, that's ten times our *total* forces!"

"Which are ill-trained, ill-equipped, and ill-regarded by our own civilians," pointed out Lefarge bitterly.

"In short, sir," said Unduma, "while we could defeat either Kolresh or Norstad-Ostarik in an all-out war—though with considerable difficulty—between them they can defeat us."

Chilongo shivered. Unduma felt a certain pity for him. You had to get used to it in small doses, this fact which Civilization screened from Earth: that the depths of hell are found in the human soul. That no law of nature guards the upright innocent from malice.

"But they wouldn't dare!" protested the Premier. "Our friends . . . everywhere—"

"All the human-colonized galaxy will wring its hands and send stiff notes of protest," said Lefarge. "Then they'll pull the blankets back over their heads and assure themselves that now the big bad aggressor has been sated."

"This note—of Rusch's." Chilongo seemed to be grabbing out after support while the world dropped from beneath his feet. Sweat glistened on his wrinkled brown forehead. "Their terms . . . surely we can make some agreement?"

"Their terms are impossible, as you'll see for yourself when you read," said Unduma flatly. "They want us to declare war on Kolresh, accept a joint command under Norron leadership, foot the bill and— No!"

"But if we have to fight anyway," began Chilongo, "it would seem better to have at least one ally—"

"Has Earth changed that much since I was gone?" asked Unduma in astonishment. "Would our people really consent to this . . . this extortion . . . letting those hairy barbarians write our foreign policy for us— Why, jumping into war, making the first declaration ourselves, it's unconstitutional! It's *un-Civilized*!"

Chilongo seemed to shrink a little. "No," he said. "No, I don't mean that. Of course it's impossible; better to be honestly defeated in battle. I only thought, perhaps we could bargain—"

"We can try," said Unduma skeptically, "but I never heard of Hans Rusch yielding an angstrom without a pistol at his head."

Lefarge struck a cigar, inhaled deeply, and took another sip from his glass. "I hardly imagine an alliance with Kolresh would please his own people," he mused.

"Scarcely!" said Unduma. "But they'll accept it if they must."

"Oh? No chance for us to get him overthrown— assassinated, even?"

"Not to speak of. Let me explain. He's only a petty aristocrat by birth, but during the last war with Kolresh he gained high rank and a personal following of fanatically loyal young officers. For the past few years, since the king died, he's been the dictator. He's filled the key posts with his men: hard, able, and unquestioning. Everyone else is either admiring or cowed. Give him credit, he's no megalomaniac—he shuns publicity—but that simply divorces his power all the more from responsibility. You can measure it by pointing out that everyone knows he will probably ally with Kolresh, and everyone has a nearly physical loathing of the idea—but there is not a word of criticism for Rusch himself, and when he orders it they will embark on Kolreshite ships to ruin the Earth they love."

"It could almost make you believe in the old myths," whispered Chilongo. "About the Devil incarnate."

"Well," said Unduma, "this sort of thing has happened before, you know."

"Hm-m-m?" Lefarge sat up.

Unduma smiled sadly. "Historical examples," he said. "They're of no practical value today, except for giving the cold consolation that we're not uniquely betrayed."

"What do you mean?" asked Chilongo.

"Well," said Unduma, "consider the astropolitics of the situation. Around Polaris and beyond lies Kolresh territory, where for a long time they sharpened their teeth preying on backward autochthones. At last they started expanding toward the richer human-settled planets. Norstad happened to lie directly on their path, so Norstad took the first blow—and stopped them.

"Since then, it's been seven hundred years of stalemated war. Oh, naturally Kolresh outflanks Norstad from time to time, seizes this planet in the galactic west and raids that one to the north, fights a war with one to the south and makes an alliance with one to the east. But it has never amounted to anything important. It can't, with Norstad astride the most direct line between the heart of Kolresh and the heart of Civilization. If Kolresh made a serious effort to by-pass Norstad, the Norrons could—and would—disrupt everything with an attack in the rear.

"In short, despite the fact that interstellar space is three-dimensional and enormous, Norstad guards the northern marches of Civilization."

He paused for another sip. It was cool and subtle on his tongue, a benediction after the outward rotgut.

"Hm-m-m, I never thought of it just that way," said Lefarge. "I assumed it was just a matter of barbarians fighting each other for the usual barbarian reasons."

"Oh, it is, I imagine," said Unduma, "but the result is that Norstad acts as the shield of Earth.

"Now if you examine early Terrestrial history— and Rusch, who has a remarkable knowledge of it, stimulated me to do so—you'll find that this is a common thing. A small semicivilized state, out on the marches, holds off the enemy while the true civilization prospers behind it. Assyria warded Mesopotamia, Rome defended Greece, the Welsh border lords kept England safe, the Transoxanian Tartars were the shield of Persia, Prussia blocked the approaches to western Europe . . . oh, I could add a good many examples. In every instance, a somewhat backward people on the distant frontier of a civilization, receive the worst hammer-blows of the really alien races beyond, the wild men who would leave nothing standing if they could get at the protected cities of the inner society."

He paused for breath. "And so?" asked Chilongo.

"Well, of course suffering isn't good for people,"

shrugged Unduma. "It tends to make them rather nasty. The marchmen react to incessant war by becoming a warrior race, uncouth peasants with an absolute government of ruthless militarists. Nobody loves them, neither the outer savages nor the inner polite nations.

"And in the end, they're all too apt to turn inward. Their military skill and vigor need a more promising outlet than this grim business of always fighting off an enemy who always comes back and who has even less to steal than the sentry culture.

"So Assyria sacks Babylon; Rome conquers Greece; Percy rises against King Henry; Tamerlane overthrows Bajazet; Prussia clanks into France—"

"And Norstad-Ostarik falls on Earth," finished Lefarge.

"Exactly," said Unduma. "It's not even unprecedented for the border state to join hands with the very tribes it fought so long. Percy and Owen Glendower, for instance . . . though in that case, I imagine both parties were considerably more attractive than Hans Rusch or Klerak Belug."

"What are we going to do?" Chilongo whispered it toward the blue sky of Earth, from which no bombs had fallen for a thousand years.

Then he shook himself, jumped to his feet, and faced the other two. "I'm sorry, gentlemen. This has taken me rather by surprise, and I'll naturally require time to look at this Norron protocol and evaluate the other data. But if it turns out you're right"—he bowed urbanely—"as I'm sure it will—"

"Yes?" said Unduma in a tautening voice.

"Why, then, we appear to have some months, at least, before anything drastic happens. We can try to gain more time by negotiation. We do have the largest industrial complex in the known universe, and four billion people who have surely not had courage bred out of them. We'll build up our armed forces, and if those barbarians attack we'll whip them back into their own kennels and kick them through the rear walls thereof!"

"I hoped you'd say that," breathed Unduma.

"*I* hope we'll be granted time," Lefarge scowled. "I assume Rusch is not a fool. We cannot rearm in anything less than a glare of publicity. When he learns of it, what's to prevent him from cementing the Kolresh alliance and attacking at once, before we're ready?"

"Their mutual suspiciousness ought to help," said Unduma. "I'll go back there, of course, and do what I can to stir up trouble between them."

He sat still for a moment, then added as if to himself: "Till we do finish preparing, we have no resources but hope."

The Kolreshite mutation was a subtle thing. It did not show on the surface: physically, they were a handsome people, running to white skin and orange hair. Over the centuries, thousands of Norron spies had infiltrated them, and frequently gotten back alive; what made such work unusually difficult was not the normal hazards of impersonation, but an ingrained reluctance to practice cannibalism and worse.

The mutation was a psychic twist, probably originating in some obscure gene related to the endocrine system. It was extraordinarily hard to describe— every categorical statement about it had the usual quota of exceptions and qualifications. But one might, to a first approximation, call it extreme xenophobia. It is normal for Homo sapiens to be somewhat wary of outsiders till he has established their bona fides; it was normal for Homo Kolreshi to *hate* all outsiders, from first glimpse to final destruction.

Naturally, such an instinct produced a tendency to inbreeding, which lowered fertility, but systematic execution to the unfit had so far kept the stock vigorous. The instinct also led to strongarm rule within the nation; to nomadism, where a planet was only a base like the oasis of the ancient Bedouin, essential to life but rarely seen; to a cult of secrecy and cruelty, a religion of abominations; to an ultimate goal of conquering the accessible universe and wiping out all other races.

Of course, it was not so simple, nor so blatant. Among themselves, the Kolreshites doubtless found a degree of tenderness and fidelity. Visiting on neutral planets—i.e., planets which it was not yet expedient to attack—they were very courteous and had an account of defending themselves against one unprovoked aggression after another, which some found plausible. Even their enemies stood in awe of their personal heroism.

Nevertheless, few in the galaxy would have wept if the Kolreshites all died one rainy night.

Hans von Thoma Rusch brought his speedster to the great whaleback of the battleship. It lay a light-year from his sun, hidden by cold emptiness; the co-ordinates had been given him secretly, together with an invitation which was more like a summons.

He glided into the landing cradle, under the turrets of guns that could pound a moon apart, and let the mechanism suck him down below decks. When he stepped out into the high, coldly lit debarkation chamber, an honor guard in red presented arms and pipes twittered for him.

He walked slowly forward, a big man in black and silver, to meet his counterpart, Klerak Belug, the Overman of Kolresh, who waited rigid in a blood-colored tunic. The cabin bristled around him with secret police and guns.

Rusch clicked heels. "Good day, your dominance," he said. A faint echo followed his voice. For some unknown reason, this folk liked echoes and always built walls to resonate.

Belug, an aging giant who topped him by a head, raised shaggy brows. "Are you alone, your lordship?" he asked in atrociously accented Norron. "It was understood that you could bring a personal bodyguard."

Rusch shrugged. "I would have needed a personal dreadnought to be quite safe," he replied in fluent Kolra, "so I decided to trust your safe conduct. I assume you realize that any harm done to me means instant war with my kingdom."

The broad, wrinkled lion-face before him split into a grin. "My representatives did not misjudge you, your lordship. I think we can indeed do business. Come."

The Overman turned and led the way down a ramp toward the guts of the ship. Rusch followed, enclosed by guards and bayonets. He kept a hand on his own sidearm—not that it would do him much good, if matters came to that.

Events were approaching their climax, he thought in a cold layer of his brain. For more than a year now, negotiations had dragged on, hemmed in by the requirement of secrecy, weighted down by mutual suspicion. There were only two points of disagreement remaining, but discussion had been so thoroughly snagged on those that the two absolute rulers must meet to settle it personally. It was Belug who had issued the contemptuous invitation.

And he, Rusch, had come. Tonight the old kings of Norstad wept worms in their graves.

The party entered a small, luxuriously chaired room. There were the usual robots, for transcription and reference purposes, and there were guards, but Overman and Margrave were essentially alone.

Belug wheezed his bulk into a seat. "Smoke? Drink?"

"I have my own, thank you." Rusch took out his pipe and hip flask.

"That is scarcely diplomatic," rumbled Belug.

Rusch laughed. "I'd always understood that your dominance had no use for the mannerisms of Civilization. I daresay we'd both like to finish our business as quickly as possible."

The Overman snapped his fingers. Someone glided up with wine in a glass. He sipped for a while before answering. "Yes. By all means. Let us reach an executive agreement now and wait for our hirelings to draw up a formal treaty. But it seems odd, sir, that after all these months of delay, you are suddenly so eager to complete the work."

"Not odd," said Rusch. "Earth is rearming at a considerable rate. She's had almost a year now.

We can still whip her, but in another six months we'll no longer be able to; give her automated factories half a year beyond *that*, and she'll destroy us!"

"It must have been clear to you, sir, that after the Earth Ambassador—what's his name, Unduma—after he returned to your planets last year, he was doing all he could to gain time."

"Oh, yes," said Rusch. "Making offers to me, and then haggling over them—brewing trouble elsewhere to divert our attention—a gallant effort. But it didn't work. Frankly, your dominance, you've only yourself to blame for the delays. For example, your insisting that Earth be administered as Kolreshite territory—"

"My dear sir!" exploded Belug. "It was a talking point. Only a talking point. Any diplomatist would have understood. But you took six weeks to study it, then offered that preposterous counter-proposal that everything should revert to *you*, loot and territory both— Why, if you had been truly willing to co-operate, we could have settled the terms in a month!"

"As you like, your dominance," said Rusch carelessly. "It's all past now. There are only these questions of troop transport and prisoners, then we're in total agreement."

Klerak Belug narrowed his eyes and rubbed his chin with one outsize hand. "I do not comprehend," he said, "and neither do my naval officers. We have regular transports for your men, nothing extraordinary in the way of comfort, to be sure, but infinitely more suitable for so long a voyage than . . . than the naval units you insist we use.

Don't you understand? A transport is for carrying men or cargo; a ship of the line is to fight or convoy. You do *not* mix the functions!"

"I do, your dominance," said Rusch. "As many of my soldiers as possible are going to travel on regular warships furnished by Kolresh, and there are going to be Double Kingdom naval personnel with them for liaison."

"But—" Belug's fist closed on his wineglass as if to splinter it. "Why?" he roared.

"My representatives have explained it a hundred times," said Rusch wearily. "In blunt language, I don't trust you. If . . . oh, let us say there should be disagreement between us while the armada is en route . . . well, a transport ship is easily replaced, after its convoy vessels have blown it up. The fighting craft of Kolresh are a better hostage for your good behavior." He struck a light to his pipe. "Naturally, you can't take our whole fifty-million-man expeditionary force on your battle wagons; but I want soldiers on every warship as well as in the transports."

Belug shook his ginger head. "No."

"Come now," said Rusch. "Your spies have been active enough on Norstad and Ostarik. Have you found any reason to doubt my intentions? Bearing in mind that an army the size of ours cannot be alerted for a given operation without a great many people knowing the fact—"

"Yes, yes," grumbled Belug. "Granted." He smiled, a sharp flash of teeth. "But the upper hand is mine, your lordship. I can wait indefinitely to attack Earth. You can't."

"Eh?" Rusch drew hard on his pipe.

"In the last analysis, even dictators rely on popular support. My Intelligence tells me you are rapidly losing yours. The queen has not spoken to you for a year, has she? And there are many Norrons whose first loyalty is to the Crown. As the thought of war with Earth seeps in, as men have time to comprehend how little they like the idea, time to see through your present anti-Terrestrial propaganda—they grow angry. Already they mutter about you in the beer halls and the officers' clubs, they whisper in ministry cloakrooms. My agents have heard.

"Your personal cadre of young key officers are the only ones left with unquestioning loyalty to you. Let discontent grow just a little more, let open revolt break out, and your followers will be hanged from the lamp posts.

"You can't delay much longer."

Rusch made no reply for a while. Then he sat up, his monocle glittering like a cold round window on winter.

"I can always call off this plan and resume the normal state of affairs," he snapped.

Belug flushed red. "War with Kolresh again? It would take you too long to shift gears—to reorganize."

"It would not. Our war college, like any other, has prepared military plans for all foreseeable combinations of circumstances. If I cannot come to terms with you, Plan No. So-and-So goes into effect. And obviously *it* will have popular enthusiasm behind it!"

He nailed the Overman with a fish-pale eye and continued in frozen tones: "After all, your dominance, I would prefer to fight you. The only thing I would enjoy more would be to hunt you with hounds. Seven hundred years have shown this to be impossible. I opened negotiations to make the best of an evil bargain—since you cannot be conquered, it will pay better to join with you on a course of mutually profitable imperialism.

"But if your stubbornness prevents an agreement, I can declare war on you in the usual manner and be no worse off than I was. The choice is, therefore, yours."

Belug swallowed. Even his guards lost some of their blankness. One does not speak in that fashion across the negotiators' table.

Finally, only his lips stirring, he said: "Your frankness is appreciated, my lord. Some day I would like to discuss that aspect further. As for now, though . . . yes, I can see your point. I am prepared to admit some of your troops to our ships of the line." After another moment, still sitting like a stone idol: "But this question of returning prisoners of war. We have never done it. I do not propose to begin."

"*I* do not propose to let poor devils of Norrons rot any longer in your camps," said Rusch. "I have a pretty good idea of what goes on there. If we're to be allies, I'll want back such of my countrymen as are still alive."

"Not many are still sane," Belug told him deliberately.

Rusch puffed smoke and made no reply.

"If I give in on the one item," said Belug, "I have a right to test your sincerity by the other. We keep our prisoners."

Rusch's own face had gone quite pale and still. It grew altogether silent in the room.

"Very well," he said after a long time. "Let it be so."

Without a word, Major Othkar Graaborg led his company into the black cruiser. The words came from the spaceport, where police held off a hooting, hissing, rock-throwing mob. It was the first time in history that Norron folk had stoned their own soldiers.

His men tramped solidly behind him, up that gangway and through the corridors. Among the helmets and packs and weapons, racketing boots and clashing body armor, their faces were lost, they were an army without faces.

Graaborg followed a Kolreshite ensign, who kept looking back nervously at these hereditary foes, till they reached the bunkroom. It had been hastily converted from a storage hold, and was scant cramped comfort for a thousand men.

"All right, boys," he said when the door had closed on his guide. "Make yourselves at home."

They got busy, opening packs, spreading bedrolls on bunks. Immediately thereafter, they started to assemble heavy machine guns, howitzers, even a nuclear blaster.

"You, there!" The accented voice squawked indignantly from a loudspeaker in the wall. "I see that. I got video. You not put guns together here."

Graaborg looked up from his inspection of a live fission shell. "Obscenity you," he said pleasantly. "Who are you, anyway?"

"I executive officer. I tell captain."

"Go right ahead. My orders say that according to treaty, as long as we stay in our assigned part of the ship, we're under our own discipline. If your captain doesn't like it, let him come down here and talk to us." Graaborg ran a thumb along the edge of his bayonet. A wolfish chorus from his men underlined the invitation.

No one pressed the point. The cruiser lumbered into space, rendezvoused with her task force, and went into nonspatial drive. For several days, the Norron army contingent remained in its den, more patient with such stinking quarters than the Kolreshites could imagine anyone being. Nevertheless, no spaceman ventured in there; meals were fetched at the galley by Norron squads.

Graaborg alone wandered freely about the ship. He was joined by Commander von Brecca of Ostarik, the head of the Double Kingdom's naval liaison on this ship: a small band of officers and ratings, housed elsewhere. They conferred with the Kolreshite officers as the necessity arose, on routine problems, rehearsal of various operations to be performed when Earth was reached a month hence—but they did not mingle socially. This suited their hosts.

The fact is, the Kolreshites were rather frightened of them. A spaceman does not lack courage, but he is a gentleman among warriors. His ship either functions well, keeping him clean and comfortable, or it does not function at all and he dies quickly and mercifully. He fights with machines, at enormous ranges.

The ground soldier, muscle in mud, whose ultimate weapon is whetted steel in bare hands, has a different kind of toughness.

Two weeks after departure, Graaborg's wrist chronometer showed a certain hour. He was drilling his men in full combat rig, as he had been doing every "day" in spite of the narrow quarters.

"Ten-SHUN!" The order flowed through captains, lieutenants, and sergeants; the bulky mass of men crashed to stillness.

Major Graaborg put a small pocket amplifier to his lips. "All right, lads," he said casually, "assume gas masks, radiation shields, all gun squads to weapons. Now let's clean up this ship."

He himself blew down the wall with a grenade.

Being perhaps the most thoroughly trained soldiers in the universe, the Norron men paused for only one amazed second. Then they cheered, with death and hell in their voices, and crowded at his heels.

Little resistance was met until Graaborg had picked up von Brecca's naval command, the crucial ones, who could sail and fight the ship. The Kolreshites were too dumbfounded. Thereafter the nomads rallied and fought gamely. Graaborg was handicapped by not having been able to give his men a battle plan. He split up his forces and trusted to the intelligence of the noncoms.

His faith was not misplaced, though the ship was in poor condition by the time the last Kolreshite had been machine-gunned.

Graaborg himself had used a bayonet, with vast satisfaction.

M'Katze Unduma entered the office in the Witch

Tower. "You sent for me, your lordship?" he asked. His voice was as cold and bitter as the gale outside.

"Yes. Please be seated." Margrave Hans von Thoma Rusch looked tired. "I have some news for you."

"What news? You declared war on Earth two weeks ago. Your army can't have reached her yet." Unduma leaned over the desk. "Is it that you've found transportation to send me home?"

"Somewhat better news, your excellency." Rusch leaned over and tuned a telescreen. A background of clattering robots and frantically busy junior officers came into view.

Then a face entered the screen, young, and with more life in it than Unduma had ever before seen on this sullen planet. "Central Data headquarters— Oh, yes, your lordship." Boyishly, against all rules: "We've got her! The *Bheoka* just called in . . . she's ours!"

"Hm-m-m. Good." Rusch glanced at Unduma. "The *Bheoka* is the superdreadnought accompanying Task Force Two. Carry on with the news."

"Yes, sir. She's already reducing the units we failed to capture. Admiral Sorrens estimates he'll control Force Two entirely in another hour. Bulletin just came in from Force Three. Admiral Gundrup killed in fighting, but Vice Admiral Smitt has assumed command and reports three-fourths of the ships in our hands. He's delaying fire until he sees how it goes aboard the rest. Also—"

"Never mind," said Rusch. "I'll get the comprehensive report later. Remind Staff that for the next few hours all command decisions had better be made by officers on the spot. After that, when we see what we've got, broader tactics can be prepared. If some extreme emergency doesn't arise, it'll be a few hours before I can get over to HQ."

"Yes, sir. Sir, I . . . may I say—" So might the young Norron have addressed a god.

"All right, son, you've said it." Rusch turned off the screen and looked at Unduma. "Do you realize what's happening?"

The ambassador sat down; his knees seemed all at once to have melted. "What have you done?" It was like a stranger speaking.

"What I planned quite a few years ago," said the Margrave.

He reached into his desk and brought forth a bottle. "Here, your excellency. I think we could both use a swig. Authentic Terrestrial Scotch. I've saved it for this day."

But there was no glory leaping in him. It is often thus, you reach a dream and you only feel how tired you are.

Unduma let the liquid fire slide down his throat.

"You understand, don't you?" said Rusch. "For seven centuries, the Elephant and the Whale fought, without being able to get at each other's vitals. I made this alliance against Earth solely to get our men aboard their ships. But a really large operation like that can't be faked. It has to be genuine—the agreements, the preparations, the propaganda, everything. Only a handful of officers, men who could be trusted to . . . to infinity" —his voice cracked over, and Unduma thought of war prisoners sacrificed, hideous casualties in the steel corridors of spaceships, Norron gunners destroying Kolreshite vessels and the survivors of

Norron detachments which failed to capture them—"only a few could be told, and then only at the last instant. For the rest, I relied on the quality of our troops. They're good lads, every one of them, and therefore adaptable. They're especially adaptable when suddenly told to fall on the men they'd most like to kill."

He tilted the bottle afresh. "It's proving expensive," he said in a slurred, hurried tone. "It will cost us as many casualties, no doubt, as ten years of ordinary war. But if I hadn't done this, there could easily have been another seven hundred years of war. Couldn't there? Couldn't there have been? As it is, we've already broken the spine of the Kolreshite fleet. She has plenty of ships yet, to be sure, still a menace, but crippled. I hope earth will see fit to join us. Between them, Earth and Norstad-Ostarik can finish off Kolresh in a hurry. And after all, Kolresh *did* declare war on you, had every intention of destroying you. If you won't help, well, we can end it by ourselves, now that the fleet is broken. But I hope you'll join us."

"I don't know," said Unduma. He was still wobbling in a new cosmos. "We're not a . . . a hard people."

"You ought to be," said Rusch. "Hard enough, anyway, to win a voice for yourselves in what's going to happen around Polaris. Important frontier, Polaris."

"Yes," said Unduma slowly. "There is that. It won't cause any hosannahs in our streets, but . . . yes, I think we will continue the war, as your allies, if only to prevent you from massacring the Kolreshites. They can be rehabilitated, you know."

"I doubt that," grunted Rusch. "But it's a detail. At the very least, they'll never be allowed weapons again." He raised a sardonic brow. "I suppose we, too, can be rehabilitated, once you get your peace groups and psychotechs out here. No doubt you'll manage to demilitarize us and turn us into good plump democrats. All right, Unduma, send your Civilizing missionaries. But permit me to give thanks that I won't live to see their work completed!"

The Earthman nodded, rather coldly. You couldn't blame Rusch for treachery, callousness, and arrogance—he was what his history had made him—but he remained unpleasant company for a Civilized man. "I shall communicate with my government at once, your lordship, and recommend a provisional alliance, the terms to be settled later," he said. "I will report back to you as soon as . . . ah, where will you be?"

"How should I know?" Rusch got out of his chair. The winter night howled at his back. "I have to convene the Ministry, and make a public telecast, and get over to Staff, and—No. The devil with it! If you need me inside the next few hours, I'll be at Sorgenlos on Ostarik. But the matter had better be urgent!"

Here is an excerpt from Book I of THE KING OF YS,
Poul and Karen Anderson's epic new fantasy, coming from
Baen Books in December 1986:

THE KING OF YS:
ROMA MATER
POUL AND KAREN ANDERSON

The parties met nearer the shaw than the city.
They halted a few feet apart. For a space there was
stillness, save for the wind.

The man in front was a Gaul, Gratillonius judged.
He was huge, would stand a head above the centurion when they were both on the ground, with a
breadth of shoulder and thickness of chest that
made him look squat. His paunch simply added to
the sense of bear strength. His face was broad,
ruddy, veins broken in the flattish nose, a scar
zigzagging across the brow ridges that shelved small
ice-blue eyes. Hair knotted into a queue, beard
abristle to the shaggy breast, were brown, and had
not been washed for a long while. His loose-fitting
shirt and close-fitting breeches were equally soiled.
At his hip he kept a knife, and slung across his
back was a sword more than a yard in length. A
fine golden chain hung around his neck, but what
it bore lay hidden beneath the shirt.

"Romans," he rumbled in Osismian. "What the
pox brings you mucking around here?"

The centurion replied carefully, as best he was
able in the same language: "Greeting. I hight Gaius
Valerius Gratillonius, come in peace and good

will as the new prefect of Rome in Ys. Fain would I meet with your leaders."

Meanwhile he surveyed those behind. Half a dozen were men of varying ages, in neat and clean versions of the same garb, unarmed. Nearest the Gaul stood one who differed. He was ponderous of body and countenance. Black beard and receding hair were flecked with white, though he did not seem old. He wore a crimson robe patterned with gold thread, a miter of the same stuff, a talisman hanging on his bosom that was in the form of a wheel, cast in precious metal and set with jewels. Rings sparkled on both hands. In his right he bore a staff as high as himself, topped by a silver representation of a boar's head.

The woman numbered three. They were in ankle-length gowns with loose sleeves to the wrists, of rich material and subtle hues, ornately belted at the waist.

The Gaul's voice yanked him from his inspection: "What? You'd strut in out of nowhere and fart your orders at *me*—you who can talk no better than a frog? Go back before I step on the lot of you."

"I think you are drunk," Gratillonius said truthfully.

"Not too full of wine to piss you out, Roman!" the other bawled.

Gratillonius forced coolness upon himself. "Who here is civilized?" he asked in Latin.

The man in the red robe stepped forward. "Sir, we request you to kindly overlook the mood of the King," he responded in the same tongue, accented but fairly fluent. "His vigil ended at dawn today, but these his Queens sent word for us to wait. I formally attended him to and from the Wood, you see. Only in this past hour was I bidden to come."

The man shrugged and smiled. My name is Soren Cartagi, Speaker for Taranis."

The Gaul turned on him, grabbed him by his garment and shook him. "You'd undercut me, plotting in Roman, would you?" he grated. A fist drew back. "Well, I've not forgotten all of it. I know when a scheme's afoot against me. And I know you think Colconor is stupid, but you've a nasty surprise coming to you, potgut!"

The male attendants showed horror. One of the woman hurried forth. "Are you possessed, Colconor?" she demanded. "Soren's person when he speaks for the God is sacred. Let him go ere Taranis blasts you to a cinder!"

The language she used was neither Latin nor Osismian. Melodious, it seemed essentially Celtic, but full of words and constructions Gratillonius had never encountered before. It must be the language of Ys. By listening hard and straining his wits, he got the drift if not the full meaning.

The Gaul released the Speaker, who stumbled back, and rounded on the woman. She stood defiant— tall, lean, her hatchet features haggard but her eyes like great, lustrous pools of darkness. The cowl, fallen down in her hasty movement, revealed a mane of black hair, loosely gathered under a fillet, through the middle of which ran a white streak. Gratillonius sensed implacable hatred as she went on: "Five years have we endured you, Colconor, and weary years they were. If now you'd fain bring your doom on yourself, oh, be very welcome."

Rage reddened him the more. "Ah, so that's your game, Vindilis, my pet?" His own Ysan was easier for Gratillonius to follow, being heavily Osismianized. " 'Twas sweet enough you were this threenight agone, and today. But inwardly—Ah, I should have known. You were ever more man than woman, Vindilis, and hex more than either."

He swung on Gratillonius. "Go, Roman!" he roared. "I am the King! By the iron rod of Taranis, I'll not take Roman orders! Go or stay; but if you stay, 'twill be on the dungheap where I'll toss your carcass!"

Gratillonius fought for self-control. Despite Colconor's behavior, he was dimly surprised at his ~~tant,~~ lightning-sharp hatred for the man. "I have prior orders," he answered, as steadily as he could. To Soren, in Latin: "Sir, can't you stay this madman so we can talk in quiet?"

Colconor understood. "Madman, be I?" he shrieked. "Why, *you* were shit out of your harlot mother's arse, where your donkey father begot you ere they gelded him. Back to your swinesty of a Rome!"

It flared in Gratillonius. His vinestaff was tucked at his saddlebow. He snatched it forth, leaned down, and gave Colconor a cut across the lips. Blood jumped from the wound.

Colconor leaped back and grabbed at his sword. The Ysan men flung themselves around him. Gratillonius heard Soren's resonant voice: "Nay, not here. It must be in the Wood, the Wood." He sounded almost happy. The women stood aside. Vindilis put hands on hips, threw back her head, and laughed aloud.

Eppillus stepped to his centurion's shin, glanced up, and said anxiously, "Looks like a brawl, sir. We can handle it. Give the word, and we'll make sausage meat of that bastard."

Gratillonius shook his head. A presentiment was eldritch upon him. "No," he replied softly. "I think this is something I must do myself, or else lose the respect we'll need in Ys."

Colconor stopped struggling, left the group of men, and spat on the horse. "Well, will you challenge me?" he said. "I'll enjoy letting out your white blood."

"You'd fight me next!" yelled Adminius. He too had been quick in picking up something of the Gallic languages.

Colconor grinned. "Aye, aye. The lot of you. One at a time, though. Your chieftain first. And afterward I've a right to rest between bouts." He stared at the woman. "I'll spend those whiles with you three bitches, and you'll not like it, what I'll make you do." Turning, he swaggered back toward the grove.

Soren approached. "We are deeply sorry about

this," he said in Latin. "Far better that you be received as befits the envoy of Rome." A smile of sorts passed through his beard. "Well, later you shall be. I think Taranis wearies at last of this incarnation of His, and—the King of the Wood has powers, if he chooses to exercise them, beyond those of even a Roman prefect."

"I am to fight Colconor, then?" Gratillonius asked slowly.

Soren nodded. "In the Wood. To the death. On foot, though you may choose your weapons. There is an arsenal at the Lodge."

"I'm well supplied already." Gratillonius felt no fear. He had a task before him which he would carry out, or die; he did not expect to die.

He glanced back at the troubled faces of his men, briefly explained what was happening, and finished: "Keep discipline, boys. But don't worry. We'll still sleep in Ys tonight. Forward march!"...

It was but a few minutes to the site. A slate-flagged courtyard stood open along the road, flanked by three buildings. They were clearly ancient, long and low, of squared timbers and with shingle roofs. The two on the sides were painted black, one a stable, the other a storehouse. The third, at the end, was larger, and blood-red. It had a porch with intricately carven pillars.

In the middle of the court grew a giant oak. From the lowest of its newly leafing branches hung a brazen circular shield and a sledgehammer. Though the shield was much too big and heavy for combat, dents surrounded the boss, which showed a wildly bearded and maned human face. Behind the house, more oaks made a grove about seven hundred feet across and equally deep.

"Behold the Sacred Precinct," Soren intoned. "Dismount, stranger, and ring your challenge." After a moment he added quietly, "We need not lose time waiting for the marines and hounds. Neither of you will flee, nor let his opponent escape."

Gratillonius comprehended. He sprang to earth,

took hold of the hammer, smote the shield with his full strength. It rang, a bass note which sent echoes flying. Mute now, Eppillus gave him his military shield and took his cloak and crest before marshalling the soldiers in a meadow across the road.

Vindilis laid a hand on Gratillonius's arm. Never had he met so intense a gaze, out of such pallor, as from her. In a voice that shook, she whispered, "Avenge us, man. Set us free. Oh, rich shall be your reward."

It came to him, like a chill from the wind that soughed among the oaks, that his coming had been awaited. Yet how could she have known?

ROBERT A. HEINLEIN